CALL IT DESIRE

ONE FOR ALL
BOOK 1

MAYA JEAN

Alpha read by JJ and Hannah

Beta read by Lexi, Brittany, and Donatella.

Edited by L.C. Valentine

Proofread by Judy's Proofreading

Cover by Books n Moods

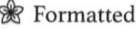 Formatted with Vellum

For Lexi,
Thanks for always calling me out on my bullshit.

AUTHOR'S NOTE

Hi! Brief note to mention that this text should not be interpreted as any sort of informational text regarding dominant and submissive relationships. What Dante and Reid enter into is fumbling and young, neither of them understanding their own dynamic yet. They are eager and want something that they don't yet have a name for, so there are elements to this story that *could* be called learning pains because they're young and not perfect. Please keep that in mind while reading.

TRIGGER AND CONTENT WARNINGS

- on-page murder
- kidnapping (not between MCs)
- torture (not between MCs)
- past drug-use & self-harm
- past death of parents
- breath play
- dom/sub dynamics
- brief mention of breeding kink
- non-sex based punishment
- possessive MCs
- mutual stalking
- survivor's guilt
- vomiting
- panic attack
- claustrophobia

PLAYLIST

- you should see me in a crown by Billie Eilish
- Vegas by Doja Cat
- Desperado by Rihanna
- Take Me to Church by Hozier
- Breakfast by Dove Cameron
- Control by Halsey
- Sucker for Pain by Lil Wayne, Wiz Khalifa, Imagine Dragons
- Criminal by Fiona Apple
- Demons by Hayley Kiyoko
- Cruel World by Lana Del Rey
- My Body is a Cage by Arcade Fire
- Romantic Homicide by d4vd
- Teen Idle by MARINA
- Bite by Troye Sivan
- Nothing's Gonna Hurt You Baby by Cigarettes After Sex
- Sweet Dream are Made of This by The Hampton String Quartet

- Trigered by Chase Atlantic
- Holding Out for A Hero by Nothing But Theives
- Dark But Just a Game by Lana Del Rey
- Run by Joji
- American Money by BORNS
- Rev 22:20 by Puscifer
- Heat Waves by Glass Animals
- Waiting Game by BANKS
- NFWMB by Hozier
- Sudden Desire by Hayley Williams
- Sail by Steve Horner
- Desire by Meg Myers
- Young and Beautiful by Lana Del Rey
- When Scars Become Art by Gatton
- Middle Of The Night by Joel Sunny
- If I Killed Someone For You by Alec Benjamin
- Movement by Hozier
- Dim the Lights by Ari Mason
- Blood in the Cut by K. Flay
- Creep by Scala & Kolacny Brothers
- Terrible Thing by AG
- Put It on Me by Matt Maeson
- Animal by Troye Sivan
- Nightcall by Kavinsky
- Bad Things by I Prevail
- Once Upon a Dream by Invadable Harmony
- Can't Help Falling in Love - DARK by Tommee Profitt & Brooke
- Call It What You Want by Taylor Swift

Spotify Playlist

PROLOGUE

DANTE

My parents were stone-faced the day I went off to college. At the time I'd assumed it was because they hadn't thought they'd ever see the day one of their children went to college, let alone on a full ride. Well, mostly a full ride, I still have to figure out a way to pay for books and shit. It can't be that hard, right? Wrong. Books are five hundred dollars for a general education course. Obviously, I need to start a business producing textbooks because that's where all the profit is nowadays.

Eastport University is nice for a college that's been around for like fucking ever. Big brick buildings that dot the downtown of Eastport, spread out so that students can walk if they want, but drive if they want to look rich. Which a lot of people do. It seems the majority of my college peers are rich. Either that or they have a side job producing textbooks.

But I can't take college for granted because my sister, Ama, had always wanted to go. It had been her dream. *I'm going to be a scientist, you just watch, Dante. Something real cool where my name goes down in history because I discovered some-*

thing no one else has ever found. As soon as I'm done driving you around town, I'm out of here. I can almost still hear her voice, still see the way her dark hair blew in the breeze as we cruised the highway with the windows down. She'd started wearing makeup around that time, cat eyes and dark red lip gloss. My black curls always annoyed me, mostly because Ama had the most beautiful, fine, shiny dark brown hair. Why couldn't I have hair like my sister? I always just wanted to be *cool* like Ama.

I kick at the concrete as I continue my way back to the dorms that I have to live in thanks to my scholarship. Yeah, I got a full ride, but it also means I'm in the dorms with a bunch of weirdos that can't afford off-campus living.

Back in my dorm that I share with this freak that clips his nails twenty-four seven, I go through the mail that I grabbed on my way up. It's mostly junk, offering me insurance on a car that I don't have. Seriously, do people fall for this? I guess so. One envelope has my name handwritten in a scrawl that looks decidedly out of place in this century. Tossing myself onto my twin-size bed, I tear it open to find a check for a thousand dollars.

Be at this location at 9 p.m. on September 28th

FAT CHANCE. My obnoxious roommate continues to clip his toenails as I stare blankly down at the invitation that's probably for something like a fight club. There's no other reason I'd be invited to some secret club. When I was still a small string bean, I was in the chess club, but that all changed the summer after puberty hit. After my growth spurt in high school, I've felt like a giant walking around. Big and broad, but everyone ignores my brain. Except for the admissions office of Eastport University.

I toss the letter into the trash and get ready for bed. Fuck, I hate living in a dorm. The communal showers are mostly empty this time of night, but it's still full of steam after so many people showering before catching some Zs. Humming to myself, I haphazardly wash my hair and body, but can't get the invitation off my mind.

I wonder if the check that was included was real? Maybe I could cash it but just not show up. After all, there were no conditions. No, I can't do that. That's *stealing*. Although, it's not stealing if there was no contract. Whoever sent it was stupid enough to hand me a check without knowing a thing about me. Hmm.

Dressed in gray sweatpants and an old T-shirt, I return to my room to thankfully find my annoying roommate sound asleep on his own bed. Every time he clips his nails, or eats noisily, or does anything infuriating, this bubble of rage grows inside me to the point I'm afraid I might commit a crime that'll get me kicked out of school.

I dig the letter out of the trash to read it again. The check is made out to me, from a limited liability company that I've never heard of. Grabbing my phone, I search the state business website but there's nothing registered to the LLC that shows who it might belong to.

I toss it back into the trash. I'm not going to do anything anyway. No point.

I turn over onto my side and stare at the picture of Ama on my side table, the perfect snapshot of who she was back then. If I close my eyes hard enough, the rage inside me goes from boiling to a gentle simmer. Ever since Ama's accident,

I've spent every waking moment blaming myself, this rage inside me with no outlet threatening to make me snap at the most inopportune moment. Rubbing at my chest, I wonder if maybe I should join the damn fight club. Maybe punching some people will relieve this constant threat of rage.

Instead of ruminating on all the ways I wish life was different, I close my eyes, and force sleep to come.

———

THE SECOND LETTER comes a week later. This time, it's after a tiring week that makes me question if this college thing really is for me. Yeah, I'm smart, but this shit is annoying. A full load of courses, and now I've got a job at this little diner washing dishes. Do I want to be doing that? No. But I need just a little extra cash to pay for all the necessities my scholarship doesn't cover. Plus, I want some money for some cool tattoos.

My teeth gnash together when my roommate is once again in the room clipping his nails. How many times does one need to clip their nails? I'd rather he just scratched his nails across a chalkboard all night.

This time I recognize the scrawl on the front of the letter. It's the same as last time.

PLEASE. 9 P.M. *September 28th. 478 Southall Rd.*

HOW DID they know I wasn't planning to come... maybe because I didn't cash the check? Oh well. This check is for two thousand dollars. I guess for one night, that's worth it.

That would cover me for the rest of the semester so that I could stop working at the diner. Or I could keep going and make *extra,* extra money. That wouldn't be bad. More money for a tattoo sooner.

Clip.

Oh God.

"Can you cut that shit out?" I ask through gritted teeth.

Patton slowly lifts his annoying face to look at me. "Stop what?"

"The nail clipping."

"I'm on my side of the room."

I clench my fingers and take a deep, calming breath. "Yes, but could you please do it in the bathroom?"

Patton tilts his infuriating head. "No. I want to do it in *here.*"

Fuck. I can't kill him. Can't punch him. All the rage inside me starts to boil up until it threatens to spill over. Maybe I need a hookup. But the last one didn't go too well. I think something is wrong with me. I'm afraid to search it on the internet too because I'm not sure I want to know so much about myself. I can get off but it's never enough. So, the idea of a hookup right now actually sounds worse than just riding out the annoyance.

I grab my earbuds from my backpack and lie down on the bed, doing my best to tune out all the annoyances that turn me into a beast. Maybe I should take up kickboxing. In high school I ran track but running doesn't sound like enough anymore for all my energy, all my anger.

I fall asleep thinking about next week, about the letter, about how easy it's going to be to make two grand if all I have to do is beat some people up.

———

A WEEK later I stand outside of the dark, abandoned warehouse miles away from campus. This is probably how I get tetanus. If I do this weekly, I'd have enough money for books, tattoos, and to send some home to help my parents care for Ama. The thought of her makes my blood go cold, makes me wish I was in a ring of people that I could take down until I was surrounded by blood.

Fuck. Time to go inside. I frown in annoyance when I step in a puddle, drenching my only pair of ancient Chucks in tetanus water. Great. The water seeps into my socks as I stomp into the warehouse, aggravated for more reasons than I can count now. My shoes squeak, alerting the three other men waiting inside to my presence. If these are the dudes I'm fighting, then this will be easy street. A pair of brown-haired twins who stand at almost my height, one in glasses, one a little more broad-shouldered than the other, and a blond guy who looks like he belongs in a frat house, not in this warehouse about to join a fight club.

"So, we fighting?" I call out.

The blond frowns at me as if I'm a giant idiot. "Why do you think we're fighting?"

"I mean, why else would I be here with two thousand dollars cashed in my bank account?"

I finish crossing the warehouse to stand beside them, noticing for the first time the laptop sitting on a table before them. The screensaver flashes in the dark of the damp warehouse, countdown bouncing around the screen. When I look down at my watch, I realize it's still a few minutes before nine, so the countdown is a timer until whatever is going to happen begins.

"I'm Parker," the leaner twin says, dark green eyes glowing in the dark behind his thick-rimmed glasses. He holds his hand out to me and I take it, squeezing his hand as hard as I can. "Nice handshake."

"Ditto," I reply with a grin.

Parker winces. "What's your degree?"

"Engineering." I look around at the rest of them. "So?"

"English Lit," Parker says, he points at his twin. "That's Jacob, his degree is in biomedical engineering. Blond God over here is majoring in math."

"Math?" I ask because that sounds awful.

"I like numbers," Blond God says with a shrug. "I'm Hayden."

I hum in disinterest and cross my arms over my chest. The countdown hits nine. Someone gasps when the screen lights up. There's no image of a person. Just a black screen with that thing that shows decibels of someone speaking.

"Thank you for being good boys and showing up," the computerized voice says. "I've chosen all of you because you have a skillset that I can use. Those skills are for me to know only. But I'd like to start a team that gives the bad people what they deserve."

"Like Robin Hood?" Parker pipes up, eyes gleaming.

The message is obviously recorded because the person doesn't stop speaking.

"Four missions a month, maybe more. A house will be provided for you to live in that's more secure than any other house in Eastport. A stipend for school. If you want to kill a bad guy, it'll be cleaned up, and you won't be caught."

Sounds like a crock of shit to me.

"Alright, well, this was fun," I say while clapping my

hands. "Story time and two thousand dollars. Any of you want to spar with me so this night isn't a total waste?"

The three other guys stare at me in confusion. Oh, they fell for it. Okay. Jacob grabs Parker and tugs him over to the other side of the room. They whisper furiously, Parker making abrupt, terrifying-looking hand motions, and I stand there awkwardly beside Hayden.

"So.... we're not doing it, right?"

Hayden bites his lip as he stares down at the laptop as if it might burst into flames at any moment. "I mean... it doesn't sound too bad? If they can provide proof to us that lets us know this isn't some joke..."

"You'll kill people?" I ask because seriously? Murder.

Hayden shrugs, fingers flexing at his sides. "If they're bad."

"This can't be real. There's no way this is real."

I take a deep breath to calm my nerves. I'm going to get tetanus and probably end up in prison because this is an undercover sting to find young men that are willing to commit felonies for some cash. Am I willing to commit a felony for cash? Crap. I am. I guess you never really know yourself until faced with the decision.

Jacob and Parker return to stand beside us again. Parker looks pleased, Jacob looks a little resigned, and Hayden looks somehow ambivalent to it all.

Jacob slowly squats down to grab a suitcase underneath the table that holds the laptop. It has a piece of paper taped to it with all four of our names. He clicks open the sides and reaches inside, pulling out manilla folders that he slowly hands to each of us, before lowering the suitcase back to the ground. Maybe it's another check?

The manilla folder holds three stark white papers. One

contains the lease to a brownstone close to school in the rich part of town, all four of our names on it. The second is a monthly recurring transaction set up to my bank account for six thousand dollars. Shit. What the hell? The third and final paper is about my sister, Ama. Who the hell is this person? How do they know about my sister? And there's no way I can turn this down if it's true.

I hurriedly slam the manilla folder shut and stare down at my shoes. My socks are still damp from outside, Converse dirty and close to falling apart. The other guys remain eerily quiet. I thought I'd be coming here tonight to get some quick cash, maybe punch a few people, get my aggression out that I can't take out on my roommate. But now I'm not so sure. The money is hard to turn down, a nicer place to live without hearing someone clip their nails literally twenty-four seven, and Ama. I am always thinking of Ama. Maybe this is worth doing just for her, to know that her future can be taken care of in a way my parents can never even dream of affording.

"I got keys for a Mercedes?" Parker says in confusion. He slowly holds up a pair of shiny keys for us to see. "Anyone else get a car?"

Hayden shakes his head, but holds up a pair of house keys. "I got keys to the house."

"Well," Jacob says blandly, gaze flitting between the three of us. "Hi, roommates."

And I guess it really is that simple. Everyone has a price.

1

DANTE

"No fucking way, dude."

Hayden aims his ocean-blue eyes at me, all squinted and shit. Fuck. "Please, Dante."

Oh fucking, fuck, shit, damn. Jacob and Parker stand off to the side of the large living room, arms crossed, identical smiles on their terrifyingly similar faces. I am so fucked.

"It's too dangerous," I mumble, already knowing I've lost the fight on this one.

Hayden's sweet smile sends a shiver right down my spine. "Please?"

"Okay, gross, don't use your *daddy, please* smile on me. It won't work. Fine. Whatever, I'm outvoted here anyway. But I am *not* cleaning blood from your jeans again because you guys are always so fucking messy." I sneer at all of them because they *are*. Slobs. "You can clean the blood out of your designer jeans by yourself. I am mostly speaking to you, Parker."

"Hey!" Parker yells with a roll of his eyes. "I do my own laundry."

"Oh, so now we just flat-out lie during the tribunal?" Jacob quips with a leer of his own.

I hold my hands out with a grunt, all of them quiet and turn to look at me. "Just shut up. Hayden, you better have a hell of a plan to get us into the back of the club and out without being noticed by a single person."

Hayden's smile is somehow even worse than it was a moment ago. Oh no. This time my stomach curdles and sweat breaks out at the back of my neck. When I glance over to Jacob and Parker, they're wearing the same sort of look that Hayden is. I grimace as I realize tonight is going to be absolute hell in more ways than one.

An hour later, I'm working my way into the club alone, already fighting the urge to cringe at the smell of sweat and alcohol. I hate clubs. I also hate leather pants but that's what I'm wearing because the guys always have to make me a spectacle. The club is warm, flashing lights adding to the bad mood the place has put me in. Now I'll also have a migraine tonight.

As eyes in the club turn to me, my body prickles with awareness of their stares. I hate being ogled. If I could fade into the background everywhere I went, I'd be a happy, happy man. I mumble half-hearted apologies to people as I bump into them while making my way to the center of the dance floor, but no one seems to care. Everyone is too caught up in their own lives.

People are either drunk or high, two things that I can't stand myself. Hayden is going to owe me something off of my wish list after tonight. I'm thinking those really expensive headphones I've been eyeing that I'm too cheap to purchase for myself. Mr. Rich Kid can buy me what I want after dressing me up in leather pants, a mesh shirt, and putting goddamn eyeliner on me.

I start to dance, raising my arms so that the shirt lifts enough to show off my stomach that's muscled and covered with tattoos. Some eyes stay on me, but the majority go back to their own business. That won't do. Fuck.

My watch buzzes with a reminder that the boys are starting the mission, but I'm not causing a big enough distraction to get the bodyguards at the doors at the other end to abandon their station. I've got to get sluttier or louder, not sure which one is the best option. My eyes scan across the crowded club, looking for absolutely anything to get me the distraction I need.

But my eyes land on a platinum-blond twink instead. Oh. He has a nose piercing, and a barbell through his perfectly shaped eyebrow. The longer I look, the more I realize his hair has streaks of rose pink shot through it. He's wearing tight-as-fuck jeans and a mesh crop top that shows off the skin of his stomach. My brain does this red-alert-cease-to-think thing when I notice the fucking ring through his belly button. Oh, Jesus Christ. The way he's moving his hips to the beat, arms in the air, eyes closed, makes my body feel like molten lava is moving through it. Now is not the time to try to pull someone.

"Are you trying at all," Parker drawls into my ear.

I growl and Hayden laughs through the comms. "You're going to piss him off. When he goes full Hulk in a rage, maybe we'll get the guards gone. Oh. Guys, this door is unlocked, oh no, oops."

"Fuck, Hayden," Jacob gasps just before the comms go dead.

That sounds bad. But I'm in the middle of the dance floor

with no further information, so the only thing I can do is stick to the original mission. Get eyes on me or cause a scene. I shake my arms out as I think of something to do, just as my eyes catch on a big, older guy trying to drag the platinum twink off the dance floor. The twink looks unsteady on his feet, eyes glassy with the classic *I took something* look and all my protective instincts go on high alert.

Pushing my way through the crowd, I stop just behind the twink and leer at the guy just a few inches shorter than me. "Does he want to go with you?"

The guy sneers. "Sure, ask him."

I tip my head down, angling it so that I can look into the twink's light blue eyes. "Do you?"

He gulps loudly, then shakes his head. I smirk at the guy who now has a visible vein throbbing in his massive forehead.

"He said no," I drawl just loud enough for him to hear me over the music.

But the guy doesn't stop. He just tries to drag the twink away, but I've had enough. I shove the guy hard until he lets go of the blond that now stands still, just slightly swaying on his feet behind me. When a fist punches me in the stomach, I laugh at the absurdity of the moment, then throw one of my own. The dude goes down with a loud crack against the dance floor and suddenly I've got the distraction I needed because all the bodyguards are rushing toward me. Oh no. Maybe this was not the guy to punch tonight.

I pick the twink up, toss him over my shoulder, and make a break for it outside as the guards chase after us. Fuck. How am I going to get out? Also, this guy isn't even fighting me which is bad news altogether if he's taken something. Goddamnit. Now I'm cursing my height because there's no way to sneak away unseen, which means I'll have to steal a car or hide somewhere else. The dead weight of the twink is not helping either.

The guard at the front door presses his finger to his ear, then narrows his eyes on me as I come to a sliding halt in front of him.

"Hey, buddy," I say with an aw-shucks grin.

The guard slides his hand to his hip, but I'm faster, even one-handed as I keep my left arm over the thighs of the twink to not lose him. One right hook later and the guard crumbles to the floor. Glancing over my shoulder, I see four other guards fighting the crowd, so I know it's time to run as fast as I can. The night air is chilly since it's autumn in Eastport. My years of track in high school really pay off as I make a break for it, totally ignoring my bike that's parked in the lot of the club. Hopefully the boys can get it home before it can give authorities a lead. Although it's registered to a dummy limited liability company, so hopefully we're fine. Fuck. Think about the matter at hand, Dante.

My head is light as I pant during my frantic run through the city streets. I spot a dark alley, and turn into it. I place the twink on his feet, carefully situating him against the damp wall to grab my phone out of my too-tight leather pants pocket. No messages from the boys and my comms are still dead. Shit.

I squeeze my eyes shut tight to blot out the irritation. I knew it would go down like this but no one ever fucking listens to me. I'm just the brawn... but sometimes I know what I'm talking about. I need to stop letting Hayden always get his way.

"Where am I?" the twink slurs, eyes narrowed to slits as he stares blankly at me.

I slap his cheek softly to wake him up more. "What's your address, so I can get you home?"

He mumbles something but I can only make out six forty-two. There are only so many addresses with that number combination in the immediate area. Wait. Maybe he has a wallet. I fumble around to reach his back pocket, but that's when he decides that I'm a danger. Lifting his arm fast, he uppercuts me and my eyes sting with tears. Jesus. Now my nose is bleeding, my phone is useless, and I've got my hand in the twink's back left pocket, not remotely in the way I was imagining back at the club. This night blows.

He slumps back against the wall, looks at me once, opens his mouth, and I have just enough presence of mind to take a step back as he hurls all over the place. Nooooooo, not my special edition Chucks. Fuck. Hayden owes me Chucks and headphones now. But at least I have hot twink's wallet. Reid —he doesn't look like a Reid. He lives at six forty-two Highland Avenue. That's not far from us and pretty close to the university.

A slight sheen of sweat covers Reid's face despite the coolness of the night. My lips bunch to the side as I bite the inside of my cheek. I hope he has a roommate or something to check on him, otherwise I'll have to take him back to our house. The fastest way for me to get murdered is bringing someone home. Parker would be livid.

I order a rideshare from an app, then do my best to gather Reid into my arms in a way that looks remotely normal. Once the ride comes, I carefully arrange Reid into the back seat, buckling him in.

He smells like really nice cologne, the kind that they keep behind the locked counter at department stores. It's sweet and spicy at the same time. I bite down harder on my cheek as the driver pulls away, his eyes glancing often in the rearview mirror no doubt thinking I'm some kind of pervert. I toss a hundred-dollar bill at the driver before hastily climbing out of the car to toss Reid over my shoulder in another fireman's carry.

He lets out a long groan as I march up the brick stairs leading to his three-story townhome. A light is on downstairs, so I don't feel too bad knocking. The doorbell at the front turns green as if someone is watching me, so I duck down with a grin and pat Reid's thighs.

"Got a delivery for you, a Reid Warton."

The light turns red, so I stand back up and try to squint through the shaded glass of the door. Nothing. A few moments later, a shadow appears and the door opens to reveal another short guy, this time with hair so dark auburn, but with the same hypnotizing light blue eyes as Reid.

"Reid? Where did you find him?"

"Uhm."

The guy winces. "Right. Can you help me get him inside? I can't carry him. I'll pay you."

"You don't need to pay me," I mumble, but the guy doesn't hear me, he's already turned around and heading back inside.

The place is outfitted with more technology than the house I share with the boys. Everything is sleek. Marble floors, dark wood stairs leading to the other floors. Reid's arms slap my thighs as I carry him up the stairs, following along behind the guy that I'm hoping is Reid's brother considering their similarities. A dark bedroom on the second floor is where I'm led, and like the good boy I am, I carefully lay Reid down on the rumpled bed. It's still dark, so I can't make out the posters on the walls, but the room has that same sweet-and-spicy smell that washed over me earlier in the car.

Some odd urge comes over me that makes me lift the blanket from the foot of the bed to cover Reid up. He quickly rolls over onto his side, curled fists tucked under his cheek, making his lips bunch as he sighs in his sleep. The platinum-blond strands of his hair stick to his forehead. Just as I reach out to brush the fine-looking strands away, someone behind me clears their throat.

I stand up straight and turn around to meet the knowing face of Reid's brother.

"You're awfully nice to bring him home."

I shift awkwardly on my feet. "I didn't want him to go home with the wrong person. Plus, he threw up on me."

He raises one eyebrow. "Cute."

I scowl. "Not really, these are my favorite Chucks."

The man's gaze lingers on my bloody nose, then lowers down to my black leather Chucks with the custom skull on the sides. His lips twitch at the corner before he slowly lifts his gaze back to mine.

"I'm Mason."

I hold my hand out for a shake, but Mason looks mildly terrified at the idea of touching my hand. Okay. I retract it and do my best to smile my real smile, not the scary one that shows too many teeth that Jacob says is my serial killer smile.

"Dante."

"Lovely to meet you," Mason says with a pasted-on smile. The smile fades as he glances from me, to his brother on the bed. "Thank you for bringing my brother home. What do I owe you? Does a thousand dollars sound good?"

Now I'm insulted. I brush past Mason to flee down the stairs. I can feel him chasing after me, so I pause at the front door with a frown. "He took something back at the club. I don't know what, but he was fucking out of it, so maybe watch out for him."

I quickly leave the house before Mason can argue further. The driver is gone, but I don't care. Our house is only a few minutes' walk a few blocks away. I realize how ridiculous I look in my black mesh shirt and leather pants, all my tattoos on display. No wonder Mason wanted to pay me. I look exactly like someone that *expects* to be paid for a good deed. By the time I get home, the house is still pitch black, so that worry I felt earlier starts to niggle at the back of my brain.

But it quickly disappears once I enter my passcode and push in through the front door. The boys all sit on the couch as they play the new video game they're addicted to with Scully sitting on the couch behind Hayden. That damn cat.

"Bro, what happened?" Jacob asks without taking his eyes off the television.

"Caused the distraction you needed," I answer, kicking my ruined shoes off by the entryway. I toss Hayden the most intense glare I can muster. "You owe me new custom Chucks *with* the skulls and the headphones on my wish list. I got puked on tonight."

Hayden rolls his eyes. "Fine."

I go to climb the stairs, then pause when I realize they're all in their boxer briefs. No fucking way. I turn around slowly to find them all sheepishly looking anywhere but at me. Even the damn cat.

"Seriously? You got blood on your jeans and came home in them again! I have told you a million times to take them off and burn them before coming home."

"They're that pair that cup my ass just right!" Hayden

argues, voice slightly hysterical. "It's just my jeans that have blood, okay. Jacob got a little carried away with this one."

I roll my eyes. "Then why are you all in your underwear?"

Parker shrugs one lean shoulder. "We didn't want Hayden to be alone when you yelled at him."

Pinching my nose, I take a deep, calming breath. "Did you at least get the money?"

"Duh," Jacob says just before angrily mashing the buttons on the controller. "We already sent it off to the rightful owners."

Well, at least they all did that right. I climb back down the stairs and stomp toward the laundry room. Once I've spent an hour doing my best to spot clean fresh blood out of Hayden's designer jeans, I trudge back up the stairs toward my room. God, I really want a shower after this shit show of an evening.

My bedroom is my haven. Dark green walls, wood floors, bookshelves along the walls without windows. The room is dark and moody, but homey when I turn the low lights on at the corners. I flip through my vinyl records for a minute, then grab one and put it on to listen to while I unwind.

After stripping off my clothes in the walk-in closet, I put them down the laundry shoot, then head into the bathroom. Bath or shower? The bath is too much work tonight despite my aching muscles. Fifteen minutes later, I step out of the shower and dry off with a fuzzy towel, then walk naked into my bedroom only to find Hayden lounging on my bed with Scully on his lap.

She really is a beautiful cat if she wasn't so pissy all the time. She seemingly *only* likes Hayden, which makes no sense considering it's Hayden. Two years ago we'd had a mission a few hours away, and when we'd returned to the townhouse, we'd found Scully clinging to the top of Parker's car as if she'd gone for the most wild joyride of her life. Of course, Hayden had saved her from the roof, so she'd imprinted on the asshole immediately. Scully pisses me off so much because I *want* her to like me, and no matter how many treats I give her, she still hisses and spits at me every chance she gets. Ugh.

"Jesus, we've talked about this." I hastily grab a clean pair of boxers from my dresser and step into them. Pursing my lips, I turn back around to glare at Hayden. "You gotta wait until I'm in the bedroom before coming in, okay?"

"Sorry." But Hayden does not sound remotely sorry. He casts his eyes low, sheepishly running his finger along my fluffy bedspread. "Are you mad at me?"

"No, Hayden. The jeans are not a big deal." I pat his head gently before tossing myself onto the bed. "Now let me sleep."

Hayden smiles a normal smile, not the scary one from earlier. He traipses out of the bedroom, Scully trailing along behind him, and closes the door with a final snick. The soft, dulcet tones of "Blues in Green" wafts from the record speakers. I close my eyes and take some deep breaths, letting the need for sleep wash over me. If someone had told me when I started college that I'd be recruited by someone to join forces to take down "bad" people, I would've laughed in their face. But, over the course of the past few years, these guys have become my family. College student by day, modern-day Robin Hood by night. Okay, sometimes we kill people, but that's pretty rare. Usually we just steal back what is rightfully someone else's. Are the ethics murky? Yes. Do I sleep well at night? Normally.

It takes a while, but finally sleep comes, and I drift off

with light blue eyes staring up at me as we dance in an empty club.

2

REID

Today started off just like every other day. Awfully. I spent the morning nursing a headache and sipping coffee at the kitchen island while Mason reamed me out for almost getting myself killed by taking illicit drugs. They didn't seem illicit when I paid for them and took them in the middle of the club, but whatever floats his boat. At least the headache isn't a migraine, thank God for small mercies.

My leather jacket barely cuts the cold wind as I walk across campus, but the aesthetics are what really matter. Black skinny jeans, black vintage leather jacket, black shit-kickers, and resting *leave me the fuck alone* face, almost guarantees me that I'll be undisturbed on my way to class.

Favorite classical music blasting in my earbuds, the day doesn't seem like total shit. Maybe it's only up from here. I've got two of my easiest math courses this morning, then I can shit off the rest of the day. If Mason isn't home at least. If Mason is home, he'll surely make me do something abso-lutely evil like clean the oven or rearrange my closet to go from shades of gray to black. The man acts like he's a decade older than me but we're only four years apart. Sure, he's somehow smarter than me, but that doesn't make him better.

I scowl thinking about Mason yelling at me earlier this morning. Who does he think he is? I huff as I redo the argument in my head. This time I snap back, tell Mason to let me do what I want, stop hovering like a freaking helicopter mom. Just because our parents are dead doesn't mean he's my mom now. He's just my brother. I don't care if he became my guardian when I was still a teen. He's not my parent. No matter how much he might think he is.

The door to the mathematics building is heavy as always, so I have to use a little extra force to shove it open. Of course, this makes me lose balance, trip over the rug inside, and spill my coffee down my pants.

"Fucking A," I curse. Taking a deep breath, I close my eyes and lift my face to the heavens.

"You're alive," someone says from in front of me.

Snapping my eyes open, I find myself face to face with the hottest man I've ever seen in my life. Dark, wavy hair that's been haphazardly styled to obscure his forehead. Almost black eyes, plush dark pink lips that have a sheen of wetness on them, and tattoos peek out from under his too-tight T-shirt. It's freezing outside and he's got no jacket on. Amazing. His eyes bore into mine, endless dark pools that root me to the spot.

"Oh." His eyes flick down to the spilled coffee on my pants. The most lethal smirk of all time tilts just one corner of his lips up. "Deja vu."

Huh? My eyebrows furrow as I stare up at him. "Do I know you?"

He blinks slowly, once, twice, and then turns his face away to look over his shoulder. A few beats go by before he turns back to me, face now a blank slate.

"No, sorry. You looked like someone I knew." He reaches out as if to touch my elbow, then seemingly thinks better of it and retracts his hand back to his side. With an awkward clearing of his throat, he steps back toward the hallway leading to the stairs. "See you around."

What an odd morning I'm having. I rush to the bathroom to wipe off as much of the coffee as I can, but it's useless because it is now a permanent part of my outfit. Better that than vomit. Wait. An odd memory niggles at the back of my brain, like a sneeze that just won't come. Infuriating. I toss my now empty cup in the trash and flee the bathroom toward my class a few floors up. The building is silent on the higher floors, as the upper-level math classes attract the more quiet sort of student. Thankfully. Probably why I chose the major to begin with over Mason's insistence that I choose one more suited to my personality.

Mason had then had the gall to suggest I get a business degree. As if he even knows me. Such a turdface. I push into the classroom just in time, the professor trailing in behind me. Normal class.

Thankfully, it's a little warmer outside when I step into the bright midday sun after both of my courses are finished. I'm still smarting from the loss of my coffee earlier. I bite my lip and wiggle my nose as the hoop through my nostril itches from the cold. I really should take it out tonight, but I've always been terrible about exactly two things: taking care of myself, and remembering to do something just before bed. Both things usually culminate in my falling asleep in the same clothes I wore that day.

It's a twenty-minute walk back home, something I'm eternally grateful for today. Less time for Mason to hound me about my bad life decisions. Might as well infuriate him further by smelling like smoke when I walk through the door. Cupping my hand to protect the cigarette as I walk, I take a deep inhale when I finally get it lit.

The burn of the smoke settles my nerves, but reminds me that all I've had today was half a cup of coffee and two bites of a croissant. God damn, I'm starved. The prickling sensation of being watched washes over me. I pause in the middle of the sidewalk, cigarette dangling from my mouth as I glance around. A few people are milling around but no one is paying a lick of attention to me, just how I like it. Must've been a phantom thought.

Taking a final drag of the cigarette, I toss it down, then hurriedly stomp it out with my boot at the base of the stairs leading up to the house. Mason will surely see it there, shining like a beacon of my descent into revelry and madness.

The hushed sounds of Mason whispering furiously into his phone draws me toward his office on the first floor. One hand pressed to his forehead, the other cupped around his mouth, he looks the picture of a distraught man. For one tiny moment I worry that something terrible has happened, but then I remind myself that the worst thing that could happen to us already has. Nothing else can hurt that bad. His gaze lifts to mine and every ounce of emotion disappears from his face. He furiously hangs up, then lifts his light blue gaze to mine.

"How was class?" Mason asks, clearly pretending to actually care.

I scowl. "Fine. Why? Having me sent off to rehab?"

Mason rolls his eyes and dramatically pinches his nose. "You don't need rehab. You need someone to care about you, which is precisely why I'm here."

"Precisely," I mock with a sneer.

Mason stares, his eyes narrowed to slits. We've always been like this, even before the death of our parents. Siblings have a one-way ticket on how to rile each other up the most. The only thing that keeps us from killing each other most of the time is the fact we're all the other has now. Also, probably the money. Committing murder surely ensures we wouldn't have access to that cushy, ever-growing pile of money to spend how we see fit.

"Reid, please stop with the drugs," Mason begs with his shoulders slumped. "It terrifies me."

I blink slowly at the sound of actual fear in his voice. My lip twitches and I look down at the ground as a surge of emotion bubbles up inside me. No. I won't feel it. The sounds of Mason standing from the chair, his soft footfalls stepping closer echo around us but I do my best to stand unmoving. No emotions. None. I can't.

"Reid," Mason whispers. He's close enough to touch, but doesn't.

I take a deep breath, squeezing my eyes shut as I count my inhales and exhales, doing my best to curb the panic threatening to choke me. All I can hear is the whistle of the air from my flared nostrils and the soft sound of Mason rubbing his fingers together, an anxious trait he's had since childhood.

"Don't ask me to make promises that I can't keep," I implore softly, soft enough that for a moment I'm afraid Mason didn't hear me. But when I look up, he's looking back at me with those eyes so identical to my own, to our mother's, that I'm afraid I'll barf up my internal organs.

Mason nods slightly. "Alright." He returns to behind the desk, his eyes now firmly on the computer in front of him. "I'll keep saving you until you tell me to stop, just so you know. We're all we have left."

"Unfortunately," I mumble, fleeing the room before I can see the heartbroken look on his face.

I spend the rest of the afternoon and evening hidden in my room to avoid Mason. Earbuds in, classical music blasting in my ears, I draw in my notebook until the world fades away. I brush the graphite on the page, hoping to smear it a little, and pull away with a small smile when it has its desired effect. Somehow I've ended up drawing the hot guy from earlier, the slight curl of his dark hair over his ears, eyes so deep they're almost black, warm glow of his skin under the black tattoos. He's committed to memory now, along with the other people in my notebook.

When my room darkens, I roll out of bed to get dressed for my evening out. I scroll through my phone hoping to find someone to hook up with, but nobody is appealing to me tonight. I'll have to find someone the old-fashioned way at the club, then traipse off to a bathroom stall for five minutes of feeling like I mean something to someone. I desperately need a trip to the salon for a touch-up of my roots. I don't want anyone to be able to tell my natural color. As far as anyone else is concerned, I was born platinum blond. The natural red of my hair makes me feel like I see my mother's face staring back at me in the mirror. The blond makes me someone else.

I pause at the floor-length mirror in my walk-in closet. Brushing my hands down my chest, taking a moment to admire how I look. My hair is artfully messy, eyes dark with the mascara I carefully applied, along with the black skinny jeans and pepper-gray concert tee. I have to admit I look worth at least ten minutes in a bathroom stall. Maybe I'll get lucky and find a guy that wants to take me home so I can feel something besides nothing for just a handful of seconds.

I wait in line for approximately two cigarettes' worth of time before getting ushered into the club without having to pay a cover. At least I'm worth that. The club thrums with music, the smell of sweat permeating the air. Something inside me settles at being just another body in a room full of people wanting. I work my way between them on the hunt for someone that could keep me distracted for the evening. Nobody fits the bill.

I won't waste the evening though. Throwing my head back, I let the rhythm of the music move me, and the pulsing beat that silences all the insidious thoughts in my traitorous brain. Hands grab my hips and sway me, but I ignore them. I even ignore the lips that move over my neck because none of them feel right. Nothing is right.

The bar is packed when I leave the dance floor for familiar territory. It's easy to push my thin body through everyone until I'm leaning against the gleaming wood of the bar, beckoning the shirtless bartender over with a flirty smile. Two shots of top-shelf vodka later and still no one at the bar is even remotely interesting. A few guys try to chat me up but they either look like minute men, or they don't smell right. If someone doesn't smell right, it ruins my entire mood.

Tonight was a waste of fucking time.

I toss money down on the bar, then work my way back through the crowded dance floor towards the exit. That odd prickling feeling crawls up my neck again, but when I turn around, there's no one looking at me. That I can tell at least.

Lighting up again, I stand in front of the club as I wait for a ride back home. Stars dot the sky, but they're muted from the light pollution of the city. Moon's still big and bright though. I squint up at the sky in wonderment and take a harsh drag of the cigarette.

"Smoking kills," a voice rumbles from behind me.

Ugh. After taking a slow, final drag, I let my cigarette flutter to the ground before stomping it dead with the heel of my black boot. Blowing the smoke out of the corner of my mouth, I turn around to aim my displeasure at the disembodied voice.

But it's him. The guy from earlier today. Except this time he's dressed in tight dark blue jeans and a sleeveless muscle tee that shows off the tattoos across his ribs. Golden skin, dark slightly curled hair, and a smile just the right side of dangerous, lighting a wildfire in the pit of my belly.

"Everything kills," I quip. I grin up at him and point at the helmet hanging from the tips of his long fingers. "Motorcycles kill just as many people as cigarettes per year."

That goads a sharp laugh out of him. "Do better with your made-up statistics."

"It's very true," I reply, despite it being total and utter shit.

"It's not. Your body is a temple and all that jazz."

"Says the guy covered in tattoos."

One dark eyebrow rises as he looks down at me. "It's art on the temple. I can show you, if you want."

"Give me a ride home and we'll see. Reid," I say, holding out my hand for him to shake.

He stares down at me for one taut, long moment, before his large hand easily envelops my own. I'm not a short guy, but he's so tall that he makes me feel small. Maybe tonight isn't a total loss.

"Dante," he replies softly.

Why does my brain feel like it already knows him? That odd niggle in the back of my brain gets worse, but nothing comes to fruition. I can't remember anything. Maybe I had a brief encounter with him at the club while cooked out of my gourd on drugs. Such a shame because I'd love to have the memory of him. I'll have to make a new one.

Dante keeps a tight hold of my hand to tug me toward the alley beside the club. A shiny, brand-new-looking motorcycle sits gleaming under the streetlight. He swings one long leg over it, then holds the helmet out for me. I stare, shocked for a moment, and step closer when he wiggles the helmet to get my attention. Dante slips the helmet over my head, then pats the sliver of space behind him. I climb on and wrap my arms around his middle. God, he feels so fucking familiar. Smells familiar too. He smells like sweet liquor and outside after a storm, two things that shouldn't go together but oddly do.

He slaps my hand softly just before the bike lurches to life. Fear rattles through me for a second until I slide closer, clinging to him like a koala. His back and stomach vibrate with a laugh as the bike navigates the almost empty roads of downtown Eastport. I hook my chin over his shoulder to watch out in front of us. He handles the bike like second nature, big, strong hands tight across the handles. I admire the veins of his forearms for one second, then shake myself loose and focus back on the road.

Somehow he navigates the bike right to my street. My heart races, blood pounding in my ears when he pulls the bike right up in front of my house. What the fuck? I jump off and yank the helmet off, angrily tossing it at his feet.

"Who the fuck are you?" I scream, uncaring about attracting the attention of my neighbors. "How do you know where I live?"

"Oops," Dante says with a look so petrified and raw, that some of my anger dissipates. Some of it. Not all of it. But some.

"Who *are* you?" I demand incredulously. I'm going to lose my shit in the next thirteen seconds.

"I brought you home last night."

I was not expecting that. I close my eyes tight to try to remember last night, but all I remember is taking a pill from some stranger at the club, then waking up in my bed this morning. This is so me.

"Listen," I say slowly, desperately needing this guy to understand. "I'm sorry if I said anything last night... anything misleading. But I don't date, okay? I'm sure we had a good time and that it was very lovely, but please do not get any ideas in your head. Also, I am just rooming here. I'm very poor. I have no money."

Dante swings his big legs off the bike and takes a step closer, forcing me to take a step back as he looms over me. "You live here with your brother."

"Jesus Christ, did you come inside for a chat? My ass is good, but it isn't *that* good."

Dante's eyebrows furrow as he looks down at me, his eyes shifting between mine. Some of his hair has fallen into his face, the odd urge to push it away overwhelms me for one halting second until I squash it down. A car honks in the distance, but neither of us reacts as we remain locked in this weird standoff. Finally, Dante swallows roughly and tears his gaze from me.

"We didn't have sex. You got high at the club, went catatonic, hurled all over my custom Chucks, and then I brought you home after finding the address in your wallet." Dante narrows his eyes at me. "They were my favorite Chucks, by the way."

Who the hell is this guy? "We didn't fuck?"

Dante shakes his head as a flush works its way over his cheeks. Interesting. "No. I'm a perfect gentleman. Your brother though..." Dante pauses and flicks his gaze up to the house, then back to me. "He offered to pay me a thousand dollars for having the decency to bring you home."

I snort because that's so very Mason. "I hope you took it."

Dante smirks. "I'm not that hard up for money. Plus, you looked pretty hot on the dance floor before the whole puking thing."

"Stop mentioning the puke," I mumble as mortification threatens to overtake me. Jesus. I meet the hottest guy on earth, puke on him at the club, and then he doesn't even fuck me. Where is the reset button?

Dante's laugh is a low rumble. "Sorry, it was just really memorable."

"Well, forget it and forget me." I turn around to go inside, head held high, but I pause at the foot of the stairs. "Why were you in the math building earlier? I've never seen you there before?"

"I had a meeting with a friend."

My eyebrows furrow. "At the math building?"

"Yes," Dante quickly replies. "Listen, don't take pills random people give you at clubs. It could kill you."

I roll my eyes. "You sound like my brother. I'm alive, aren't I?"

Dante's smile shatters me. "For now, maybe not the next time." He takes a step forward, reaches into my pockets, and deftly tugs out my phone. He flips through it for a few seconds before carefully sliding it back into my pocket. "Call me if you ever change your mind about that dating thing."

"No fucking for fun allowed?"

Dante grins, slow and sweet, and dips so that we're eye level as he whispers, "Sweetheart, if I fuck you, I'm not letting anyone else touch you ever again."

My breath stutters in my lungs. Dante walks away with all the swagger of a man that just dropped an atomic bomb on an unexpecting someone. The roar of the motorcycle filters through the static in my brain. My fingers twitch at my sides as Dante slips the helmet on, curls his fingers in a wave, then disappears in a flurry of movement down the street.

The light is still on inside the house. I follow the sound of the television to find Mason sitting with a cup of tea, curled up on the couch like a cat. His eyes flicker from the television to me, surprise etched across his tired face.

"You're home early," Mason notes tiredly.

I roll my eyes and kick off my boots. Tossing myself down on the couch beside him, I put my feet on the coffee table knowing it'll piss him off. But his look stays soft, not remotely angry as I raise my eyes to his.

"The guy that you tried to pay off the other night brought me home."

Mason's lips part in shock. "The same guy brought you home *again*? How was his nose?"

I tilt my head in confusion. "His nose?"

"Yeah," Mason replies, eyes distant in memory. "He had a bloody nose, looked like someone got him good."

Huh. I don't reply to Mason, instead focusing on the old television show playing on the screen. The plot thickens. Dante brought me home after finding me at the club, I puked on him, and he had a bloody nose. The urge to grab my phone and ask him about his nose is strong, but I ignore it. I'm not going to waste my time encouraging someone to have thoughts about me that they shouldn't.

After all, he called me sweetheart.

But my heart is anything but sweet.

3

DANTE

Two weeks later and my nose still feels like Reid took a hammer to it. Standing in front of the foggy bathroom mirror, I tenderly push at the side of my nose with the tip of my finger. Fuck, it hurts. I don't think Reid broke it, but he definitely did something. In a way it's a nice little badge of... something that I can carry with me.

The kitchen smells like muffins when I finally swagger in. I ignore the murmur of Jacob's voice and zero in on the coffee pot. Score. Grabbing my mug with black cats on it, I fill it up, grab a warm muffin, and slink over to the table in the corner. I'm scrolling mindlessly through my phone when Hayden makes his arrival.

"Good morning, boys," Hayden says with his usual drawl. His eyes narrow in on where Jacob stands leaning against the kitchen counter, apple in hand, dark hair disheveled. "I didn't know you were home. Thought you were off with that girl. What's her name...?"

"We broke up two months ago," Jacob deadpans.

Hayden sniffles pitifully. "Right. Anyway, where's your doppelganger?"

"Miss me?" Parker calls from right behind Hayden.

Hayden rolls his eyes. "No."

The familiar sound of them sniping at one another filters over me while I chew at the muffin Jacob probably woke up early to bake. After almost four years in each other's pockets, they're the closest thing to family I allow myself to have these days. Although Hayden can be purposefully irritating, he's the smartest and best of all of us. Though Jacob will likely never admit that.

"Do we have our next job yet?" Jacob asks, eyebrows wiggling playfully at Hayden.

Hayden presses his fingers to his temples. "Hold on, I'm communicating with home base. Let me see. Nope, nothing yet."

The scowl on Jacob's face almost makes me giggle. I look back down at my phone to continue the mindless doom scrolling that's become my morning routine. And that's enough of that. I push back from the table, grab my backpack, and start the short walk to the basement garage.

Parker has always been the one I've been closest to, mostly because he tends to be quiet like me. We can be together, not say a word, and still probably call each other best friends. In the way where you call someone your best friend, but you talk to them once a year while playing catch-up. Still ride or die, we just have shitty communication skills. Also, during our slapshot self-training freshman year, I developed a little bit of hero envy at how easily Parker took to handling a gun. It's like an extension of him. Hand Parker a gun and he'll find five people within two hundred feet and shoot them dead between the eyes.

I yelp when Parker steps out in front of me, a very undignified sort of sound, and aim a deadly sneer his way. But Parker is Parker, so he only crosses his arms with that odd little smirk on his lips, perpetually messy hair falling into his eyes.

"You came home late last night," Parker notes.

I narrow my eyes on him. "Are you keeping tabs on me?"

"No," Parker lies right through his teeth. "But your bedroom was dark when I went to bed and I heard you slinking in after midnight. If you don't want to be heard, you should wear better shoes."

"Do NOT insult the Chucks!"

Parker grins, all teeth. "Where *were* you?"

I push past him, shoving my shoulder into his with too much force. "Maybe I have a separate mission from the rest of you."

Parker follows after me, huffing and laughing at the same time. I fight the flush from climbing up my cheeks because yeah, I wouldn't be the one to get a solo mission. Only Parker gets solo missions. I don't care though. I can hack into government agencies like the rest of them. I just usually get lumped into being the brawn, being the muscle so that the rest of them can do the dirtiest work.

"Dante, be real here."

I spin around so fast that Parker almost bumps into me. He lifts his hands up in defense, eyes wide as I glower down at him. "Fuck off, Parker."

A shout from the kitchen as Hayden and Jacob get up to their usual fighting tugs Parker's annoying attention off of me. Thank God. I swipe my jacket off the hook by the door, then skip down the front steps. Campus is only a fifteen-minute walk, so sometimes I forgo the bike, instead needing the exercise to clear my head on the way to class.

Five minutes into my walk, something doesn't feel right. I pause in the middle of the sidewalk, hand buried in my jacket, eyes narrowed as I scan the mostly empty street. I'm being watched. Instead of drawing more attention to myself, I keep heading toward campus, but remain aware of that niggling feeling.

The street goes from brick townhomes, to older historical buildings that contain the majority of campus. A chilly breeze washes over me as I stomp toward the engineering building. The shape of a very familiar body catches my gaze, freezing me to the spot for the second time today.

Reid casually leans against a large oak tree on the sidewalk just outside of the engineering building. The cigarette between his fingers is almost down to the filter as he takes a deep inhale, slowly blowing the smoke up into the sky with an elegant tilt of his head. Fuck. When he brings his face back down, his eyes find mine, and a small, irritatingly sexy smirk tugs at the corner of his lip.

Reid gleefully taps the side of his nose. "How's that feeling?"

My eye twitches. "My nose is fine, thank you." I mimic drinking alcohol with my hand. "How's that feeling?"

Reid's lips bunch at the side as if fighting a chuckle. "I haven't taken any pills from strangers lately if that's what you're asking."

"That's good."

Reid easily pushes off the tree, tosses the finished cigarette to the ground, and stomps it out with his heel. A flash of the creamy skin of his stomach makes me almost squirm, but I hold fast, instead staring down at him in feigned indifference.

"It seems someone has told most of the dealers to not sell to me anyway," Reid notes with a curious edge to his voice.

"Pity," I lie, because it was definitely me.

Reid taps his chin thoughtfully. "Someone's been stalking me too. Following my steps, making it impossible for me to hook up."

"Oh no."

Reid steps close enough that I can feel the heat radiating off of him, smell the cigarette smoke and the soft tinge of his musky cologne. My eyes rake over his face, the slight dark roots beginning to show at his scalp. He makes an aggrieved sound, bringing my attention back to his face. Reid presses two fingers to my chest and pushes all the while scowling up at me.

"Stop cockblocking me."

I grab his fingers with mine, twist, and tug him closer until his body is pressed against mine. "No."

Reid's chest heaves in anger and his eyes narrow. "I don't know who you think you are, but stop stalking me, stop fucking with my life, and stop pretending like you give a shit."

"Maybe I do give a shit."

"I puked on you," Reid argues with a feral snarl.

I smile down at him. "It was kind of cute."

Reid somehow just gets angrier. "I ruined your Chucks."

"Chucks are replaceable."

"Ugh." Reid twists his arm out of my grip and backs out of my reach. "You know, two can play this game. I've been watching you for the past few days."

"Oh?" That does catch me by surprise because Reid is

pretty easily the most important thing on my radar as of late. I can't imagine him having the ability to watch me without me knowing. The confusion must show on my face because Reid smirks up at me, bright blue eyes sparkling with the glory of a win.

"I can cockblock you too, ruin your night."

I shrug and brush past him, letting my arm drag across his midriff despite feeling the sudden urge to toss him over my shoulder just at the touch of his skin against mine. Not sure if I want to take him over my knee or put him on his knees.

Slipping my phone out of my jeans pocket, I navigate to my solo text with Parker. I do not need this one in the group chat.

> Need you to watch over someone for me.

> My cover was blown

PARKER

Oh?

I don't have time for this but also tell me more

> Guy from the nightclub when you guys fucked up your designer jeans again

PARKER

Hayden fucked up his designer jeans

> Okay

PARKER

You'll owe me

Okay

PARKER

Stop replying just okay

I'm not doing your laundry

PARKER

Let me borrow those leather Chucks, the ones with the roses on the soles.

WHAT THE FUCK WHY

PARKER

They go with an outfit of mine. Let me. Then we'll have a deal.

Fine

Do not fuck the mark. He's mine.

PARKER

Oh?

Stop saying oh

PARKER

Oh?????????????

Fuck off

I'M irritated all through class. Irritated at Reid, irritated at Parker, irritated at Hayden for not having another mark for us. I want to finally *do* something important in one of our goddamn missions. I want to be more than just the hot tall guy covered in tattoos that either causes a distraction or seduces someone. I was brought on to the team because I can hack without a single trace, but no, Hayden always does the hacking because he has the inability to delegate. Also, I'm pretty sure Hayden thinks we're all stupid, but most of all, me.

Which is ridiculous. If we're basing intelligence solely off of looks, then Hayden, Mr. Frat Guy Looks, would be the stupidest. But he's just a control freak and relegates me to the bottom of the barrel so I can never get any of the glory.

I get paid the same as them, so I don't know why I care so much.

Whatever.

Once my classes are over, I'm still irritated, and doubly so when it's warm enough outside that I have to carry my jacket instead of wearing it. So now my backpack is slung over one shoulder, phone in hand, and jacket draped over one arm. That nagging feeling of being watched is gone which hopefully means Reid is back at his house, instead of following me around. Not that I minded being followed, I just can't protect him if he's the one watching me.

Parker is waiting for me when I enter the house. "Give me the shoes."

Ignoramus. I punch him in the stomach and continue to walk into the kitchen. I'm starving. Parker limps behind me, and when I turn around, he's clutching at his stomach in agony.

"You are such a dick. You didn't have to use full force."

"That was half force."

"No fucking way," Parker wheezes.

During our training freshman year—training in the loose sense of the term meaning we went to the gun range, had some kickboxing, and spent time in each other's pockets so that we could work together as a team—Parker and I were always paired up. It was the two of us fighting each other, the two of us as lookouts, the two of us trauma bonding over the loss of a family member. Parker might be more deft with a weapon, but I can still knock him on his ass with a single blow.

The fridge is half empty since we haven't gone shopping in probably a few weeks. Means it's my turn. Because sometimes I'm the only one that drags themself to the store, even though Jacob is the one more apt to cook. Shit, they're all jerks. I spend a few moments tossing a sandwich together and grab the bag of chips I keep hidden in the cabinet over the fridge. Parker squawks behind me when he realizes what I've hidden. None of them can reach up there without a chair, so it's where I hide all the good junk food.

"You fucking dirtbag! You seriously hid the sour cream and onion over the fridge?"

I lift a chip to my mouth and crunch it slowly as Parker glowers at me. I toss myself down onto the kitchen table to eat my snack. Parker tosses himself down in the chair opposite me with an agonized huff. I flick the bag across the table so that he can have a few, which seems to instantly mollify him. Nice.

"Reid found out I've been doing some friendly stalking," I admit, pushing the remainder of my sandwich across the table for Parker to eat.

He takes a grateful bite, eyes narrowed my way. "What's your obsession with this dude?"

I shrug because I really don't know the answer to that. He's hot, yeah, but I could easily find a hookup. Seeing someone so reckless with their own safety has always turned on my own protective instincts. There's this obvious pain hidden deep in Reid's eyes that begs for someone to keep him safe. He might've caught me, but Parker can keep him safe when I can't be there. For now.

"I'll cover him tonight. He lives like two minutes down the street."

"I know."

Then I flee to my bedroom because I'm suddenly out of words. I've never been much for talking, actions say more than words ever can. Thankfully, the guys mostly leave me alone when they realize I've reached my quota for the day. I finish up my homework in the shelter of my bedroom, take a long shower while doing my best to not think about Reid, and end up in bed before nine in the evening. A perfect night.

I must've fallen asleep early because the loud vibrating of my watch wakes me up. Fuck. Usually I take it off before falling asleep so alerts don't disturb me. But Parker's caller ID in my phone makes me bolt upright in bed. Double fuck.

"Yeah?"

"Hey, so I have a little problem," Parker says, voice oddly high-pitched.

"What?"

"Can you come to the Double Up on the other side of town?"

I freeze while tugging a shirt over my head. The Double Up? What the fuck is Parker doing at a gay bar when he's not gay. Wait.

"Reid is at the Double Up?" I screech into the phone.

Parker wheezes slightly. "Yeah. Please hurry."

The night is dark when I peel out of the basement garage on my bike. Everything blurs around me. I don't even know if I stop for red lights. By the time I arrive at the Double Up my heart is racing and my tongue is thick in my mouth. A line still curves around the corner of the loud, thumping club, but I bypass it and head straight for the bouncer.

One hard stare from me has Tony letting me through with a bite of his lip. Easy. The hallway is dark and the smell of sex and alcohol permeates the air. Jesus. Clenching and unclenching my fists at my side only helps so much since I'm about ready to pummel the shit out of someone. Couples are hidden in the corners when I finally break into the main part of the club. Full dance floor, too-loud music, and my eyes flick over the crowd in hopes of finding Parker. But his ruffled dark hair and broad shoulders are absent from the dance floor.

I push through the swaying crowd, already irritated with the idea of having to sort this mess out. People try to tug me into a dance but I shrug everyone off, too eager to find Parker. Also, Reid. My blood boils at the idea of him at the Double Up, with someone in the bathroom, bent over the sinks with his hands pressed to the mirror.

I'm going to commit a felony.

Finally at the other side of the dance floor, I work my way into the hallway that leads to the bathroom. My heart pounds at the idea of what I might find. But thankfully, I spot Parker pretty fast. He's tucked into a shadowy corner, lean body pressed hard against the wall, with Reid leaning against him, hand tucked against Parker's side under his shirt. Rage like I've never felt before simmers under my skin. I suddenly know what they mean when someone says they saw red, because my entire vision shimmers crimson at the idea of Reid's bare skin touching Parker.

"I gave you *one* fucking order," I growl at Parker as I carefully shove Reid off of him, curling my fingers tightly around Reid's slim arm.

"Told you," Parker murmurs.

"What?" I ask, gaze flicking between them.

Reid breathes in slowly, eyes going from annoyed to irate. Oh no. I slowly slide my gaze back to Parker with trembling lips.

"You could've given me a heads-up that this was an ambush."

Parker shrugs and weasels his way away from the wall to slip back toward the dance floor. "This is between you two. I'm going to get a drink and see if any hotties will flirt with me."

"Don't lead anyone on!" I call after him.

Parker flicks me off over his shoulder as he disappears around the corner back out into the thrumming club. Reid yanks his arm but my grip is too tight, so I tug him closer until we're staring each other down.

"What are you angling at?" I roar, pleased when Reid flinches.

"I told you to stop following me, so you send your friend? What the fuck? I'm not that special!"

The way Reid says the last sentence has my alarm bells ringing. His eyes won't meet mine, instead they stay focused over my shoulder. Crimson blooms over his sharp cheekbones, his lashes sweep across his soft skin as his gaze goes downcast.

"You like breakfast?"

Reid's gaze snaps up to mine. "What?"

I clear my throat awkwardly. "There's this diner a few minutes from here. Has the best French toast of all time. Want some?"

"Do I want French toast?" Reid repeats as if I'm speaking a foreign language. Maybe I am. At least to him.

"Yeah."

Reid is eerily still for a few beats before nodding slightly. A win is a win. I let my hand glide down his arm to tangle our fingers together. I don't miss the shocked look on his face even as he tries to angle his face away from view. It's easy to guide Reid through the crowd because everyone parts for my giant-ass self. Parker leans against the bar, shot glasses littered in front of him as an adoring crowd tries to capture his attention.

He looks over his shoulder as if feeling my stare and shoots me an up-nod when I flick a wave his direction. Once we're outside the bar, Reid seems to second-guess his easy acquiescence to join me as he tries to tug his hand out of my grip. But I don't let go.

I climb onto my bike again like I did all those nights ago. Holding my hand out for Reid, it takes a few minutes, but finally he puts his hand in mine so I can drag him closer to the bike. Once the helmet is over his head, I smile up at him, but he only tilts his head in consideration. Probably not my genuine smile, then.

Reid climbs onto the back like he belongs there, easily wrapping his arms around my waist to hold on tight. The bike rumbles to life. Light pollution ruins the night sky, but a few stars still illuminate the darkness, along with a few blinking satellites. Reid is warm against my back as I swing into a parking spot across the street from the diner.

The glow of the diner sign flickers neon-bright in the dark, causing Reid's almost white hair to have shades of pinks and purples. He holds the helmet out to me and lets out an irritated huff when I don't immediately take it. I grab it from him a little more forcefully than I need to, earning me narrowed blue eyes in my direction.

"You should have two helmets with how often you've got someone riding bitch on your bike," Reid snarls before abruptly turning and marching toward the diner.

"You're the only person that rides bitch on my bike!" I call after him.

Reid pauses in the empty street, shoulders up to his ears. But he doesn't turn around, just keeps on walking, strolling into the diner like he owns the place. I bite back a smile as I follow along behind him a few beats. He's already seated by Mandy when I step through the door. Mandy's lips are fighting a laugh and her brown eyes dance with the promise of teasing later. Great.

"Hey, Mandy," I greet her.

Sliding into the booth, I let my foot tap against Reid's, and he shocks me when he doesn't immediately yank it away.

"Same as usual?" Mandy asks in her sweet southern drawl.

I hold up two fingers. "Yes, please."

Mandy disappears toward the counter with her silver hair swinging as she walks.

Reid kicks my foot, hard. "Explain yourself."

"Is that how you speak to someone?"

"It's how I speak to you." Reid rolls his hand in the universal sign for *go on*. "I'm waiting."

"Yeah, I was following you."

Mandy pops back by with two mugs and a carafe of black coffee. I watch as Reid pours three creams and two packets of sugar into his cup before taking a giant gulp. Jesus. I pour the coffee into my cup, sans creamer and sugar, and take a sip of the coffee that could power a small neighborhood. Once Mandy is gone, Reid leans forward with his elbows firmly planted on the table. My heart beats a little faster when he licks his pink lips, making them go a deep, dark pink under the sheen of his spit.

"No one else has ever ridden bitch on your bike?" Reid asks, completely throwing me for a loop.

"Uhm. That's seriously your next question?"

Reid shrugs, hair tumbling into his eyes. "Sure, why not?"

"I don't typically take hookups out of the club and I'm not letting any of my friends wrap their thighs and arms around me," I explain before taking another sip of my coffee.

Reid leans back with a thoughtful look on his face. "Why have you been following me?"

"You're reckless."

"That's not your problem," Reid snaps. The fury that radiates from him doesn't irritate me, doesn't make me want to snap back, it only makes me want to get beneath it to see what he's like under all that snark. His behavior is a security blanket.

"It's not. But I like to protect people. It's kind of a job, if you will."

Reid snorts. "Like neighborhood police."

"Sure." I lean forward on my elbows this time, dipping my gaze until Reid is forced to meet my eyes. "Why are you at a different club every night taking drugs from random strangers?"

A hot blush creeps up Reid's neck and cheeks at my question. He's silent for a long while, but I don't break his gaze.

"I like to feel like I'm in danger," Reid quietly admits, tongue peeking out to lick at his plump upper lip.

"There are better ways to do that."

"Yeah?" Reid asks hopefully, perking up in his seat.

"Sure."

Reid narrows one eye at me in obvious suspicion. His eyes

stay on me even when he lifts the mug to his mouth to take another borderline comically large gulp of his sugary hot bean water.

"My parents died in a plane crash when I was a teen," Reid announces with all the gravitas of someone saying the sky is blue. Just facts. He swirls his finger over the edge of the mug, eyes caught on the movement of his finger. "Do you remember that plane crash that happened because the manufacturer cut corners when making that model of plane? The CEO of the flight company knew and was in on it with the manufacturer... blah blah blah buying planes for cheaper to increase profits. Anyway, my parents were on the flight that crashed into the Rockies. My brother and I got a settlement, enough for us to be okay for the rest of our lives, but I should've been on the plane with them."

"What do you mean?"

Reid squeezes his eyes shut tight. "They were going to visit my uncle but I didn't want to go... because... I don't like my uncle. He's not a good man. He's a senator and believes that everyone not like him deserves to die. My parents left me home alone... Mason was away at college, so my parents let me stay behind. I was a teen and I was old enough."

I can see the moment Reid shuts down, the moment the conversation is too much for him. His shoulders push back and his weary gaze lifts to mine. Mandy returns just in time to save us from a talk I'm not sure Reid really wants to have. We eat silently, Reid picking at his breakfast. By the time my plate is clean, Reid's cleared half his plate and a few bites of his egg. I stare at him, hoping to maybe encourage him to eat, but all he does is glower down at his half-eaten food like it's personally offended him.

"If I chase danger enough, maybe it'll find me," Reid finally admits as he pushes his plate away.

"Doesn't work like that."

Reid's eyes sparkle as he leans forward, close enough I can feel his breath fan across my face. "It does though. You found me."

I slap a couple of twenties on the table and stand fast enough to make Reid gasp. Grabbing his bicep, I yank him out of the booth, ignoring his annoyed huff because at this point I don't give a shit anymore. The night is cool when we step outside, but warmth blooms low in the pit of my belly as Reid fights against my grip. Little does he know, I like that shit.

"Stop," I order in the lowest voice I can.

Reid freezes like a deer caught in headlights. I slip the helmet over his head, straddle the bike, and manhandle him onto the seat behind me. He grips my stomach tight without me urging him to do so. I keep thinking about him dancing in the club, taking pills from some random person. By the time we pull up in front of his house, my blood is boiling again, but not in the way I'd expected.

Reid jumps off the bike, grabs the helmet off his head and angrily slams it to the ground. He's one second away from screaming my head off when I grab him by the shirt, and plunder his mouth with mine. One second is all it takes for Reid to get with the program. His fingers curl into my hair, tugging me closer as I all but lay claim to his mouth. He tastes like the goddamn sugar-laced milky coffee back at the diner. The way his lips move against mine ignites a fire at the base of my spine. Everything blurs around the edges when Reid presses close, lifting a leg as if trying to straddle me on the bike.

"Invite me inside," I mumble against his mouth.

"What are you, a vampire?" Reid snarks back.

Fuck. Tangling my fingers in his hair, I yank his head back until he gasps with pleasure or pain, I can't tell either way.

"Invite. Me. Inside," I order, enunciating each word with a tug of his hair.

"Come inside," Reid dutifully repeats.

I smile in the dark. "Good boy."

Reid all but melts against me. I've found his trigger and I'm the bullet.

After that bone-melting kiss, Reid is easy to maneuver into the house. The lights are off and the house is quiet when Reid unlocks the door. He gathers himself enough to press a slim finger to his lips in the universal sign to shush. I bite the inside of my cheek to keep from laughing. Reid points at my shoes, then points at his own as he carefully takes them off and places them on the mat by the door. I didn't have to do this last time but who gives a fuck. I copy him, toeing my shoes off and leaving them on the mat.

I follow quietly behind Reid as we climb the stairs to his room. I like being in his house better this way. My eyes trail from the top of his head, down to the perfect curve of his ass. We sneak quietly into his room and Reid shifts behind me to close the door, locking it before pressing his forehead against the wood. He stays quiet as he moves around the room, clicking on the fairy lights pinned to the ceiling. The room glows to life, dark blue walls and a large queen bed piled high with comfy-looking blankets.

Reid fiddles with his phone before tossing it onto his desk as music softly booms from the speakers in the corners of the room. It's a sensual beat, undoubtedly meant for fucking. But I don't need a soundtrack when I fuck.

I nod toward the rug in front of me. "Get on your knees."

Reid's jaw firms up and I half expect him to argue. But that kiss earlier must've rattled his brain enough to make his normal argumentative nature calm. He falls to his knees in front of me, eyes hooded as he lifts his gaze to meet mine. Fuck. He's so pretty. I clench my hands at my sides to keep from reaching out yet. Not yet.

"I'm not normal," I say softly. I never know how to explain this part well. How sometimes I like to cause pain to my hookups, sometimes I like to make them cry, and that's why I don't usually have repeats. So, I have to say this clear as day so that Reid understands what I need... what I want from him.

Reid swallows loudly. "Okay."

"Sometimes I like to make my partners do what I want. I like to make them cry. Do you like to cry, Reid?"

Reid's chest heaves with each breath. His hands lift from his thighs as if he's going to reach out, then fall back to his thighs, firmly gripping at the muscle under his tight jeans.

"I'm really bad. All the time."

Fuck. The way Reid says it breaks my goddamn heart.

I've got to do this right.

If I mishandle Reid, I'll hurt us both.

And something about Reid needs protecting.

I'm the only one who can keep him safe.

4

REID

My heart pounds away in my chest like a runaway stallion. I've been chasing danger for years, playing Russian roulette with my life to see how many times I can tempt fate before it finally takes. Now I've got this dangerous god standing over me with the fires of hell in his eyes. How did I get so lucky?

Dante screams danger, but something primitive inside me knows that he would never actually hurt me. Not enough to kill me. Maybe just enough to give me unbridled pleasure. I'm rotten to the core. Maybe Dante can replace everything decaying inside me with something good, something worthy of desire.

"I'm not an expert at this," Dante mumbles, a small sliver of doubt filling his eyes. He rubs his face with one hand while placing the other atop my head, fingers gently working their way into my hair. "Green means good, yellow means slow down or give me a minute, and red means stop. If I do something you don't like, you say red immediately. I'll stop everything, no questions asked. Got it?"

"Yeah."

"Just so we're clear, you hold the real power here. You know that, right?"

I blink slowly up at him because I don't understand. I've got no power. He's standing over me, all six foot plus inches of him, two hundred and some pounds, all dark eyes and tattoos, I don't feel like the powerful one when on my knees.

"I don't feel powerful," I mumble.

Dante sweeps his hand down my face, thumb pressing against my mouth until I open it and take his thumb inside. His skin tastes salty and it's warm when it presses against my tongue until I open my mouth further. My jaw aches a little, but it's worth it when Dante's eyes go even darker.

"We really should work this out outside of the bedroom," Dante says, voice raw and dripped in need. "But I don't have the patience to wait any longer."

"Fuck me?" I ask breathlessly.

Dante shakes his head. "Not tonight."

I move to stand, suddenly pissed off, but Dante replaces his hand on top of my head and holds me down. Being held down lights me up and everything blurs again. Dante's smile is small and mean as he sees my reaction. My eyes track Dante's other hand as he reaches into his back pocket, tugging out his wallet, then fumbling one-handed for a condom. Irritation sweeps through me at the sight of the foil packet.

Dante shushes me when he notices my reaction again. "Just for tonight, we'll get tested so we don't have to use condoms from now on, okay?"

I nod slowly even though I'm pissed that tonight I won't get to taste him. My thighs ache where I press my fingers into them. The pain settles while I watch Dante unbutton his jeans and push them down enough to slip his semi-hard cock out of tight boxer briefs. I sway a little closer but his fingers in my hair hold me from veering close enough to touch.

He rips the foil with his teeth, then clumsily fumbles to get the condom on with one hand, all so that he can keep his other hand firmly on top of my head. Saliva pools in my mouth just at the sight of Dante's cock. Once his dick is encased in the condom, he steps in a little closer, his fingers curling in my hair to tug my head back slightly. His cock slaps against my lips in a clear demand for me to open further. The heat in Dante's eyes makes the base of my spine tingle and a shiver rolls through my body.

"Can I choke you on my cock?" Dante asks, voice thready.

I nod eagerly, no longer able to form words. He slides his cock in slowly and I moan at the way it fills my mouth. I could do without the taste of latex, but it's only for tonight, that's what he promised at least. Everything in my brain goes silent when Dante thrusts deep into my mouth without any warning. My eyes water and I lift my gaze to his once my nose is buried in his groin. I swallow around him, enjoying the warmth of him on my tongue, loving the way all my nerves settle as I'm giving him pleasure.

The way Dante looks like he's perilously hanging on to control sends another shiver through me, this time from the need to see him lose said control. It seems when I'm a brat, when I push boundaries, that makes him go crazy. So I lift my hands from my thighs to grab his hips tight and take him somehow even deeper into my throat, until I can't breathe through my nose from how close it's pressed against his warm, musky skin.

"Fuck, you little brat," Dante swears from above me.

If I could grin with my mouth full of cock, I would, simply

because of the reaction I elicited from Dante. Tears form in my eyes and slowly slip down when I can't catch my breath at all. I'm choking on his cock and I love it. Dante tugs painfully at my hair to slide himself halfway out of my mouth, then he slams back in and holds there so that I can't get my bearings at all. He repeats it over and over until I'm convinced there's no air left in my body. My head is floaty and my body vibrates as Dante takes his pleasure from my mouth.

He swears softly, groans, and then I feel him swell against my tongue as he comes with a low growl. I close my eyes tight to imagine his taste, imagine the warmth of him sliding down my throat. He'd tell me I was a good boy then, surely he would. I'm bad every single moment of the day, but I can be good when I'm on my knees for Dante.

Dante pulls out of my mouth, letting go of my head. I fall to my hands when he steps away to get rid of the condom. I feel loopy in a way I've never felt before after sex. Almost like I could sleep and cry at the same time. Dante reappears just in time before I crumble to the ground. He scoops me up in his arms and manhandles me to the bed. I can't even fight him.

Feeling out of my body, I distantly watch him tug his jeans all the way off, then remove his shirt one-handed, which is sexier than it has any right to be.

"I'm gonna take care of you, Reid," Dante says as he joins me on the bed.

My limbs are loose and weak, making me feel like a rag doll when he takes my shirt off, then my own pants. He tugs me against the curve of his body and takes my mouth in a toe-curling kiss. I hadn't even realized my heart was racing until it slowed under the onslaught of his lips. Dante's kisses are all-consuming. No one has ever kissed me the way Dante kisses me, like I'm his sole focus, like the whole point of his existence is to take me apart with his mouth.

When his hand wraps around my cock, my entire body detonates. Warmth rushes through me as I shake from my orgasm. It feels like flying. Dante's mouth presses close to my ear as I float down from the most intense orgasm of my life.

"I've got you, you're alright," Dante murmurs over and over again.

His hand still gently cups my softening cock, but I can't feel remotely embarrassed about it. I just need him to keep touching me. A quiver rolls through me, followed by another one, until I realize I'm shaking like I'm coming down from a fever. Dante swears roughly and removes his hand from my cock, making me mewl at the loss of his warm touch. Bundling me up in his arms again, he quickly crosses my bedroom to push into the bathroom. He sets me on my feet but doesn't stop touching me even as he fumbles with my shower.

I blink slowly and he's tugging me along with him to stand under the warm spray of the shower. Oh, that feels lovely. Between the hot water and the warmth of Dante's skin, the shivers stop and my mind quiets once again. That's nice. Dante's hand tenderly pets down my back when I slump against him, unable to hold myself up one moment longer. I've never had a hookup take care of me like this afterward. Usually, I suck or fuck and get left alone immediately after. Works better for me that way.

Dante turns the shower off, then proceeds to tenderly dry me off. I can't meet his gaze, so I keep my eyes trained on the wet floor under my feet. Strong arms swoop me up again. I let myself be carried into the bedroom, let myself be gently laid on the bed, even let Dante curl up behind me, cradling me close to his strong body. He smells like chai tea and my woodsy body wash. It works.

His lips press against my neck, forcing my eyes closed in a rare sense of comfort. Who am I? In Dante's arms there is danger, but there's also an odd sense of freedom that I can't really explain.

"Do you feel better?" Dante asks softly, fingers rubbing just under my belly button in a maddening motion.

"Mmm," I hum, unable to speak full words.

Dante gently leans his forehead against the nape of my neck. "I wanna give you what you need, but I don't know if either of us knows what we need. No more clubs, okay? No more drugs."

"We're not dating," I mumble, voice sounding slurred to my own ears.

"That's okay," Dante says roughly. "That's okay. You can still be mine, Reid."

"I can?"

"Yeah, for a little while. I'll be your fix. No more clubs."

"No more clubs," I promise just before sleep overtakes me.

———

SOFT, early morning sunlight slashes across the comforter when I blink awake. I'm curled up on my side, something hot and alive pressed against my back. The night returns to me in shattered pieces, like glass on a subway floor. I'd gone to the club to seek out a hookup, knowing that someone had made it impossible for me to get laid and also to get any sort of illicit drugs. I'd known that either Dante would show up, or whoever was tailing me would barge in.

But I hadn't thought Dante would be everything I needed.

And also everything I fear.

Needing someone only leads to heartache because everyone leaves, always.

He's still asleep against me, giving me time to snoop through his phone. He has facial recognition, so I lift the phone enough to get a glimpse of his sleeping face. Easy peasy. Well, we aren't dating, but are fucking, so it seems smart for me to have a way to track him. I pull up a web browser and type in the IP that'll get to the backend of my laptop. Downloading the tracking application that I created for Mason, I install it on his phone, then hide it among a clutter of other applications that I doubt he even uses. Just when I'm about to start digging through his photos and emails, he lets out a snore that sounds kind of like he's waking up. Shit. I toss the phone where it was and feign sleep.

Dante moves against my back, curling against me as if he wishes he could tug me inside himself. I fight against the urge to lash out at his clinginess, because in a way I sort of need it. Last night was... I'd never felt so out of my body before. Transcended to another dimension.

Dante pulls back enough to roll me onto my back, his eyes quickly zeroing in on mine. Whatever he finds on my face pleases him because he smiles a dopey sort of smile. But then it vanishes when his gaze trails over my bare stomach. I grab the sheet and tug it over me so that he can't see my skin, he must've not been paying attention last night.

"Where did you get those from?"

"None of your business," I snarl. The loopy, lovely feeling from last night is now gone. Time to flee. Before I can even attempt to get out of the bed, Dante is tugging me closer, looming over me until all I can see is his dark hair and eyes.

"It's my business now." Dante presses down against my body with his own when I try to wiggle out from under him. His fingers wrap around my throat, gently squeezing until I still. "Where did you get those scars?"

"Me."

Dante's nostrils flare as he seemingly processes my admission. "No more."

"You can't take away all of my coping mechanisms and expect me to be a fully functioning human," I say around a bitter laugh. He's got to be joking. I can't fuck randoms at the club, can't take pills and dance the night away, can't cut myself when my emotions get too big, too hard to handle. What the fuck am I supposed to do?

"You've got me now," Dante argues, eyes never leaving mine.

His fingers curl tighter against my throat until my lips part and I gasp to get some air into my lungs. My heart races again, this time at the threat of danger from his fingers, and from the shock of being told what to do.

Dante squeezes his fingers tighter while swooping down to kiss me. If I wasn't already lacking oxygen, I'm definitely suffocating when he fucks my mouth with his tongue. Everything quiets under his touch.

A phone squealing breaks the moment and forces Dante to tug away from me.

"Fuck," Dante swears, lips swollen and eyes oddly haunted.

I lie still as he rolls over me to grab at his phone, only calming once his phone is in his hand. He has a privacy screen, so I can't spy from this angle, which is mildly depressing, but his face tells more of a story than reading his text messages ever could. Dante goes from irritated to pissed in just a few seconds. He pinches his nose for a brief moment, before climbing out of bed to quickly get dressed.

I take in the miles of tattoos on his back that move with his muscles as he bends down to put on his pants. It's a desert scene, cactus, the rising sun, mountains blocking the view. No doubt it took a lot of time. And his arms are filled with one-off tattoos that shouldn't work together but somehow do. He's hot as sin, and for a little while, he's mine. My nosiness wants to know what each tattoo means. Another time, I guess. Maybe. If he isn't a huge liar. Half of me expects to never see him again. The idea of that sends some weird pang through me.

"I have to go," Dante says, tugging his shirt over his head.

"Oh."

He runs a hand through his messy hair, somehow managing to make it even worse.

Once fully dressed, he returns to the bed to hover over me. Before I can utter a word, he swoops down to kiss me hard on the mouth. The kiss isn't sexy or soft, it's claiming. With one single kiss, Dante says who I belong to. My lips tingle when he pulls away.

"You've got my number. Text me so I have yours." Dante's eyes sweep over me, at least across the skin that's still visible over the sheets. His lips curl up in an approximation of a pained smile before he leans down to bite my bicep. Pain lances through me, but he's gone before I can even manage a return attack. That fucking *hurt*.

Wrinkles pop at the corner of Dante's eyes. "You're mine."

He flees my bedroom with a pleased pep in his step. Suddenly, I regain my senses in his absence. I hurry to pull on the sweatpants and hoodie that lie forgotten on my floor. I'm still tugging on the hoodie when I bust out of my room and fly down the stairs two at a time.

Mason shouts at me from the kitchen, but I don't care. Dante is just opening the front door when I shove him hard, making him let out a little *oomf* as he crashes into the door.

"What the fuck?" Dante swears as he turns around. "If you break my nose again, I swear to God..."

"What?" I screech, voice at the same decibel of a grieving medieval woman.

Dante looks unrepentant. His fingers rub at his nose, pulling away to check for blood. Jesus. I broke his nose and puked on him? This dude has a serious death wish when it comes to me, but I'm supposed to be the one with a danger kink? I think not.

"You didn't break it," Dante mumbles, shifting from foot to foot. "You just... broke some blood vessels, okay. That's not the point. Why did you shove me?"

Why did I shove him? It's forgotten now. He looks like a puppy as he stares down at me with those dark eyes, brown hair disheveled and falling onto his forehead. Maybe he gives me cute aggression. Instead of answering with useless words, I lean up on my tiptoes and kiss his nose.

We both stare at each other in shock when I pull away.

"What's going on here?" Mason calls from behind us.

I look over my shoulder to find Mason with a coffee mug in hand and a frown on his face. Fuck.

"Nice to see you again," Dante says casually.

"Likewise." Mason's eyes flit to me. "I didn't realize you had a guest."

"It was just..."

"We're dating," Dante announces, then pushes me away and flees out the door. Oh my God, that motherfucker.

"Oh?" Mason says with wide eyes.

"We're... that's not... he just..."

"He seems sweet. You puked on him, broke his nose, and he brought you home to tuck you in. You could do much worse, Reid."

I glower at Mason's back as he swings around to return to the kitchen. Maybe I should tell him that Dante likes me to literally choke on his cock. I doubt he'd be saying I could do much worse then.

Sundays usually mean Mason and I spend the day avoiding each other in the townhome. This is best done by Mason working in his study, while I hide away in my room to sketch. No reason to break tradition now.

I isolate myself in my room with coffee and a croissant that I pick at for the better part of the morning. I draw Dante again, but this time with the familiarity of someone who's kissed the mouth they're drawing. He has a sweet Cupid's bow that's hard to capture, but I do my best. The broad sweep of his shoulders reminds me of old Superman cartoons, the triangle of the shoulders to the thin waist. Dante has the perfect body, made for strength and danger. But my drawings don't do him justice.

I never texted Dante like he told me to, mostly because I'm not convinced I'll see him again. The urge to do something reckless, something stupid eats away at me, but maybe just in case he does come back, it's worth behaving. Just a little.

Mason knocks on my door around dinnertime.

"It's fine," I call out. Our universal code for permission to enter a room.

The smell of homemade chicken soup fills the room, making my mouth water and stomach gurgle with hunger pains. Mason's smile is soft when he sets the hot soup down on the nightstand beside my bed. There's a glass of orange juice and some toast as well. I swallow loudly, then lift my gaze back to Mason's.

"Thank you," I say softly.

Mason's lips twitch at the corners. "You're welcome. Are you staying home tonight?"

I drop my gaze back to my desk, only then just realizing my sketchbook is still open. Slamming it closed, I rub my fingers over the supple leather cover.

"Yes. I don't think I'll be going out much anymore."

"Oh?" Mason asks with one curious eyebrow raised. "That's good. We can watch some football if you like or something on a streaming service. Whatever you want."

"Yeah... I'll come down after I eat."

Mason grins and backs out of the room. I eat slowly as I type out a text message to Dante. My finger hovers over the send button for a while before I gather the courage to tap it.

> You have my number now. Happy?

SECONDS later my phone screen illuminates with a message.

> DANTE
> Immensely. I'll text you tomorrow.

I SMILE DESPITE MYSELF.

5

DANTE

"Mission tonight," Hayden reminds us all as we scarf down dinner. "We'll meet in the garage at nine."

Jacob cooked jambalaya that made the whole house smell like sizzling herbs and spices. Sometimes when he cooks something extra delicious before a mission, I wonder if he knows we're all going to die and that's his kind send-off. But it's probably more he's anxious and that's how he deals with it. I won't complain about it though. His cooking is delicious.

"What's this one again?" I ask because at some point, all the missions started to blur together.

"Apparently that medical facility off highway 32 is testing on animals, but also stealing studies that undergrads are doing at the university and passing it off as their own. We're stealing the data back, not the animals!" Hayden shouts just as Parker is about to interrupt him.

Parker slumps down in his seat, distraught at not being able to save the animals. Soft-hearted jerk. He pushes his glasses up his nose, the steam from the jambalaya making them fog. We finish dinner in peace, then disappear into our rooms to get ready for the mission. I dress in my typical all black with the gun harness strapped over my chest. I jog down the stairs to slip on my new lucky Chucks, the replacements Hayden bought me, that are all black with flames dancing up the sides.

"The skull ones are better," Parker notes as he finishes snapping on his watch. Dressed in tight black dress pants and a black fitted dress shirt, he looks like he's going to a fancy ball rather than partaking in some slightly, probably shady criminal activity.

"The skull ones got puked on and have an odd yellow tint on them that I can't get out."

Parker sighs in misery for me. "Sorry, buddy."

"Whatever. These are fine too."

Parker and I stand side by side while we wait for Jacob and Hayden to join us. It's always been easiest with Parker. Yeah, we piss each other off, but I think we understand each other the best, despite Parker and Jacob being a matching set. Parker likes to kill, but only does it for good. I like to kill, but only evil people that deserve it. It's pretty much the same thing. Although sometimes I think that Parker would happily kill, even if we weren't involved in the missions. There's something inside of him that frankly scares me sometimes, but I love him like a brother, so I'd defend anything he ever did wrong.

Hayden comes down the stairs first, golden-blond hair perfectly styled in this weird slicked-back way that I could never accomplish with my slightly curled ends. He's dressed similarly to me, but with a tight, almost sheer black T-shirt. Must be cold because his nipples are like ice. Jacob's nostrils are flared as he follows behind Hayden, fingers carefully hooked into his own harness.

Hayden is the best up-close shooter of us, although I'll never admit that out loud. He can kill someone in a second flat as long as he's got his silencer on him. Jacob and Parker are the sharp shooters, able to shoot from an extreme distance. Whereas I just do whatever I have to do to get the job done. Hands, fists, guns, whatever, as long as the bad guys are defeated and we can complete the mission.

"So, simple, we get there, you and Jacob handle the security or medical personnel still there, while Parker and I get the information off the computers inside." Hayden holds out the iPad he carries around that contains enough information to put us all away for life. "Robin requests we don't kill anyone on this one since it's high profile, it'll be in the news soon."

"Wait." I look from Jacob to Hayden, and neither of them will meet my eyes. "Why is Jacob with me? Usually he's with you."

Jacob *always* has Hayden's back. That's just the way we're always paired up. Parker and I are on kill duty while Jacob and Hayden get the goods, that's the way it is, the way it *always* goes. But the tension in the air is thick enough that I could cut it with a knife and have a nice-sized dinner. When no one says anything, Parker claps his hands with something between a grimace and an awkward smile.

"Let's get going," Parker announces with false cheer.

Hayden sighs from deep in his soul. "Just do what I say, Dante. Stop asking so many questions."

I glare at the back of Hayden's head as we make our way toward the car. At least the seating sticks to the pattern. Parker drives, Jacob sits up front, while Hayden and I are squashed together in the back. The stereo starts blasting angry alternative rock when Jacob clicks into the playlist we all contribute songs to on a rotating basis. Half the time it's rock, the other half of the time it's classical music, depends on the mood when the song was added by one of us.

I lean my head against the window as the city blurs by, wondering what Reid is doing, wondering when I can see him again. Now is not the time to be thinking about him. I've got to get my head in the game so I don't end up shot, or worse, my Chucks getting sullied again. Even the thought of my vomit-covered Chucks makes me smile.

"Oh my God, why are you smiling?" Hayden asks, voice fearful.

I scowl. "I'm not."

"You were." Hayden cocks his head at me. "And it was scary, don't do it again."

Parker looks in the rearview mirror at me, eyes calculating, then he reaches out to turn the music up to drown Hayden out. Thank God. When we park around the corner of the medical facility, my heart starts to race like normal with typical pre-mission jitters. A brief thought of Ama passes over me, her smile when I got taller than her, when she said she could still beat me up even though I was bigger than her now. That pang of missing her hits me again, making my heart skip a quiet beat, just in time for us to park.

Time's up.

We all take a moment to sit there, silently hyping ourselves up for the mission. In a synchronized movement, we all tug masks over our faces in case we leave people alive, which is always the hope in a retrieval mission.

Hayden hops out of the car first, with Jacob following a close second, obviously pissed at Hayden's inability to care about his surroundings or safety. One day Hayden is going to get himself killed. He's worse than Reid in that way. Parker and I shrug our shoulders at each other when we climb out of the car, then go around to the back to join the other boys.

The facility looks exactly how I expected. Big, white building with lots of bright lights that make it seem like it could moonlight as a car dealership if it didn't have that weird something-nefarious-is-being-done-here feeling radiating from it. Hayden squints one eye at the facility, then the other, licks his finger and holds it up to the sky. Parker huffs in frustration before nudging Jacob in the back.

They're all children.

Jacob points at the entry point. "Cameras are angled in a way that only catch the edges, so if we walk right up and in the front door, we won't be seen if we keep our heads down. Don't look up."

"That's what he said," I tease, because I can never read the room.

Parker sucks his teeth and clears his throat. "Jacob and Dante, you'll take down the two security guards out front, tie them up, then I'll bring the one employee still in the back up front for you to handle while Hayden and I focus on the assets."

"No murder," Hayden reminds us.

"Yes, Dad," Parker replies.

Hayden glares at him while Jacob makes an aborting, slashing kind of movement with his hand. I am truly too exhausted to understand all of the layers of dynamics that are occurring right now. I just want to punch someone like I was promised. Tired of the shenanigans, I breeze past them all and jog across the street. The stars are blotted out today, clouds covering the night sky, and the harsh bright lights of the medical facility make me want to sneeze. But I keep my head down and walk right up to the doors. The soft sounds of the boys' footfalls echo behind me, letting me know at least they've got my back.

I stop at the front door because I didn't think this through. "So, do I knock or?"

"Jesus Christ," Hayden mumbles. The rustling of his hands over his clothes reaches my ears, just in time for him to step in front of me with gloved hands to open the doors wide.

"Hey!" a security guard shouts, but falls to the floor when Parker leans over me with his tranquilizer gun. The other guard falls shortly after in a heap of messy limbs.

"Forgot about that," I tease Parker with a smile.

He carefully rearranges his dress shirt cuffs. "I didn't. No, you can't use the gun."

"Fine," I sneer because this has been a year-long fight. Only Parker gets to use the tranquilizer gun because he's convinced the rest of us will either shoot ourselves or the wrong person.

Hayden and Parker disappear into the back, just for Parker to reappear with a man that has a gag in his mouth and the fear of God radiating out of his eyes. Amazing. I'd probably feel the same way too if Parker was manhandling me with crazy eyes. Parker disappears again while I hover over the guy who's shaking at our feet, the two security guards still out cold.

Jacob leans against the check-in desk, fingers flexing a few times out of restlessness.

"Doesn't Parker usually get brawn duty with me?" I ask from the corner of my mouth.

Jacob snarls. "I don't want to talk about it."

Ah, that's code for he pissed Hayden off again.

Hayden quiets over the comms just in time to breeze through the door Jacob and I have been standing guard around. Parker plods along behind Hayden with a pointed look in Jacob's direction. Oh he's in *serious* trouble if his twin is also pissed at him. Now I'm fucking curious.

Once we've all climbed into Parker's loaded SUV, we peel out of the alley to head back to the city. Hayden curls over his laptop as he uploads whatever data he stole. A frown etches his perfect face for only a moment, before that delighted grin spreads. That means success.

"All done. Can we stop for ice cream?"

Jacob snorts. "It's one in the morning."

Hayden clenches his jaw. "I want ice cream."

Jacob swears and looks out the window, but not before making some hand motion to Parker to indicate we should stop for ice cream. I tug my phone out as we drive, checking my text message thread with Reid. We've been texting nonstop the past week since I haven't had time to see him again. I'd watched him on campus for a brief moment. He'd had a cigarette dangling from his mouth while angrily marching toward the math building.

He's surly and argumentative in text, the same as he is in person, but he's also more apt to share details of his life. The last text from him was an hour ago, saying he was going to bed. Attached is a photo which is new. When I click into it, my heart races and my mouth goes dry. It's a simple drawing of hands wrapped around a throat, but I know that's my hand because of the tattooed phases of the moon across my knuckles.

Which means that it's Reid's throat that the fingers are wrapped around.

I'm not going to get hard in the car with the boys that are essentially my brothers-in-arms. I lead a cursed existence. The SUV comes to a stop at a gas station on an abandoned street. Before I can ask what's up, Jacob jumps out of the car and heads inside. Hayden sits beside me, arm leaning against the window with his chin resting on his palm.

Hayden's eyes dance as he carefully tracks Jacob's movement in the store, never once losing sight of him. The grin that overtakes his face when Jacob reappears is somehow both terrifying and heartwarming. More people should experience the thrill of ice cream after a theft.

Jacob tosses two pints of mint chocolate chip ice cream at Hayden, then signals with his hand for Parker to keep going. The rest of the car ride is mostly silent, except for the sound of Hayden eating his beloved ice cream. A few minutes from home, Hayden leans over the console to hand Jacob the half-eaten pint and plastic spoon. Oh, these fools. I bite back a chuckle when Jacob takes the offered ice cream. By the time we return home, the carton is empty and both boys are smiling.

Hayden trudges into the house with Jacob hot on his heels.

"Do you think they know?" I ask Parker while we wipe down the car.

Parker lifts his head with a confused sort of look. "Know what?"

"Obliviousness is genetic, I see."

I leave Parker in the garage to shower off the night. At least there's no bloody laundry to do this time. After my shower, I curl up in bed naked, and pull up my phone. How can a hand-drawn picture of me choking Reid be so fucking hot. I wish it was still early enough in the evening for me to go over to Reid's place, sneak into his room, take him fucking apart piece by piece. Instead, I send Reid a screenshot of my STD panel as a good morning present.

———

THERE WAS NO REPLY from Reid when I woke up. I try to not think too much of it. I've got two classes on Tuesdays, both senior-level required engineering courses. The autumn air is crisp when I step out of the engineering building in the early afternoon. Behind the building is a small quad that students use to study between classes.

I head that way out of instinct, some unknown force telling me it's not yet time to go home. My instinct pays off when my gaze immediately lands on Reid. He's sprawled out on a blanket in the quad, all by himself, sketchbook on the ground with a graphite pencil caught between his slim fingers. As if feeling the weight of my stare, his gaze lifts to search me out. A small private smile graces his lips when his eyes land on me.

He wiggles his eyebrows slightly, then returns to his sketchbook. I stomp over, toss my backpack to the ground, then join him on the blanket big enough for two. I wonder if he planned this, but surely not, since there's no way he knows my course load. And his next class isn't until this afternoon. I know his courses, of course.

"You're here early," I point out.

Reid lifts one hand. "You're not going to pretend you don't have my class schedule memorized?"

I shrug. "What's the point?"

Reid rubs at the paper with the edge of his dainty pinkie. "I know your schedule too, just so you know. You think I really sit out here daily in the quad wearing tight jeans that perfectly shape my ass?"

"I hope not."

His eyes practically roll back into his head. "You're delusional, but cute, so I give you that."

"You didn't reply to my text," I whine.

Reid rolls his eyes again, but this time he scoffs as well. He pulls a sheet of paper from the back of his sketchbook and hands it to me. Our fingers brush as I take the paper, forcing a vivid red blush to paint his creamy cheeks. Mmm. I hold Reid's most recent STD panel in my hands showing a clean bill of health.

I clear my throat awkwardly. "No condoms, then?"

"Whatever you want," Reid replies.

"We should talk through what we both want."

Reid hums absentmindedly as he continues to sketch in his notebook. A breeze blows over us, carrying the scent of Reid toward me. God, he smells fucking delicious. I want to eat him up. Want to hurt him too. If he'll let me.

"I like breath play, obviously," I say softly, careful of people around us.

Reid snorts. "You don't say?"

"I like to mark and bite. I also like to control. What I say, you do, unless you color out. I don't do fake rape, it doesn't turn me on, but I like to fuck hard and make you oversentitive, maybe try for multiple orgasms. Edging is great too. None of that daddy-and-boy crap, we're the same age. I just want you to do what I say and enjoy it. Also, not averse to public sex if you need it."

Reid mostly ignores me, just continues to draw. For some reason, that sets me on edge, makes me feel the need to keep talking.

"I won't let other people touch you, not while you're mine. No drugs and no self-harm."

Now I feel like an idiot with the way Reid is just continuing to sketch, totally ignoring everything I'm saying. I can feel my eyes start to twitch with annoyance. My fists clench and unclench of their own accord, looking for something to grab, or someone even. The sun breaks through the clouds, making Reid's almost white hair glow golden for a moment, despite the hints of light pink throughout. I want to bury my fingers in his hair and yank, make him cry, make him beg for me to take him hard until he can't think of anything but me. Only ever me.

Reid finishes his drawing and tosses the sketchbook into my lap. It's us. Reid is face down in the bed, face lost in pleasure with tears streaming down his face, as I loom over him, my fingers digging painfully into the meat of his thighs.

"Is this what you want?" I ask, almost out of breath.

Reid supports his chin with his hand, giving me the most disarming smile possible. That urge to make him cry overwhelms me again.

"I only bottom," Reid whispers. "You can call me princess, call me slut, call me a piece of shit, I don't really care. Just make me feel used."

Fuck. "You liked it when I called you a good boy, though."

Reid looks away from me then. After a few moments of stilted silence, Reid abruptly sits up, snatches the sketchbook from me, and shoves it into his backpack. Okay, what did I say? Was it the good boy? I stand up to chase after him, but he just rolls up the blanket and shoves it into his backpack.

"I want to come to your house tonight," Reid says matter-of-factly. "I'd rather not let Mason hear me crying during sex."

Oh. "Yeah, yeah that's fine. I'll text you my address."

Reid nods quickly, but keeps his gaze averted from mine. He starts to walk away, but I grab his wrist and tug him back to me. Uncaring about the people around us, I dip down to press a hard kiss to his mouth. Reid gasps softly, but opens up for me like the good boy that he is.

When I pull away, I place a soft kiss on his forehead. Reid still refuses to look at me, even as he marches away. I watch him go toward the math building, gaze never leaving his back. It's worth it when Reid finally looks behind him, only to find me still watching. I lift my hand to wave and can't hold back a borderline maniacal grin when he scowls at finding me still staring.

———

I SPENT the better part of the afternoon cleaning the house. The guys aren't dirty, but they're not exactly the most organized men on the planet. Clean sheets on my bed, freshly cleaned bathroom, and all the supplies I might need on the nightstand. Parker is reading a book in the corner of the sofa while Jacob and Hayden sit in the living room playing their newest video game. Scully is asleep on the back of the couch, little paws curled up tight under her face. I wish I could pet her, she makes me so wildly sad by refusing to love me back.

Deciding to keep Reid a secret from the boys was probably my best decision. But also my worst, because there's nothing like a secret to make them curious. When the doorbell rings, Jacob drops his controller and stares at the door like it could be a wolf. Yeah, we never get visitors.

"Are you expecting someone?" Hayden asks with a curious tilt of his head. Scully wakes and jumps from the back of the couch to perch beside Hayden, her green eyes narrowed toward the door.

I mime zipping my lips which does absolutely nothing to

dissuade their curiosity. I push the sleeves of my henley up higher to showcase my forearms. When I swing open the door, Reid is effortlessly putting a cigarette out on the stoop. His eyebrows wing up at the sight of me so put together, but otherwise he shows no emotion.

"Hi," I say quietly.

"Hello," Reid echoes. "Can I come in or?"

"Yeah, sorry."

I grab Reid by the arm and tug him inside, trying to hurry past the living room. But Reid digs his feet in to stare at the boys on the couch.

"You're in my differential equations class," Reid announces to the room.

Hayden grins. "Hi, Reid."

Reid's eyebrows furrow. "You know my name?"

"Of course," Hayden admits with that weird, predator-like smile of his. "I know everyone's name."

"Weird," Reid mumbles. "Kitty?"

"That's Scully," Jacob tells Reid, face turned to look down at the cat that hates his very existence. Because Scully has epic timing, she hisses at Jacob, then jumps from the couch to come investigate Reid. I expect another hiss, maybe her tail going up to warn Reid off, but all Scully does is rub against Reid's leg once, then disappear toward the back of the house to bathe in the sunlight streaming through the sliding doors.

That's enough of that. I wave at the guys and drag Reid with me toward the second floor. The moment I've got him in my room, I cover his mouth with my own. Reid squeaks a little, but otherwise gets with the program. His fingers curl into my shirt, tugging me closer until I'm almost stepping on his toes. He tastes like the fucking cigarette he just smoked and cherry hard candies.

Reid pulls away from me to take off his leather jacket. He unceremoniously drops it on my desk, then bends over to look at the framed photos on my desk.

"Your sister?" Reid asks while tapping at a framed photo.

My throat gets tight at the mention of her. I stride over and flip the photo face down. Absolutely no crying is allowed in the room right now unless it's Reid.

"Yes."

Reid lifts one delicate eyebrow. "Sore subject?"

"Yes," I repeat.

Reid tilts his head like a predator, studying me, but this is one thing he won't figure out just by staring through me.

"Get on your knees," I order, but I'm not even remotely convinced from the shake in my voice.

Reid snorts inelegantly and ignores my command. He peruses my room like an FBI profiler, looking for clues that'll tell him why I'm so willing to make him cry, make him hurt. But nothing in my room is going to tell him the motivation behind my willingness. Because there isn't any. I just like what I like, and I like Reid. If giving him pain keeps him coming back to me, then I'm more than willing to do it.

My cock hardens when Reid carefully toes off his shoes, then undoes the button on his jeans. He doesn't go any further than that though. He strides over to the bed, all long legs, and thin limbs. Nobody should be that hot, just casually sitting down on the edge of my bed like they didn't ask me to make them cry earlier.

"Well, Dante?"

"You need to spend the night here afterwards," I order while hastily yanking off my shirt.

Reid's eyes flick over my chest, taking in the tattoos that litter my skin. My body prickles under his stare and warmth blooms in my belly when Reid's gaze drops to my hard cock pressing against the zipper of my jeans. He licks his lips, then swallows loudly.

"Why do I *need* to spend the night?"

"Fucking you the way you want is going to spike your adrenaline, then it'll crash. You need to be here so I can take care of you." He doesn't need to know that I need it too, maybe even more than he does. If he left without me taking care of him, holding him, I'd be sick for days after. It happened *once* with a guy from a hookup app and I'm still not quite over it.

Reid scoffs at my demand but doesn't argue. Mostly because I think he really liked how I took care of him the other night even though he doesn't want to admit it.

"Lie back." I motion for him to lie down. "I'm going to take your pants off."

Reid lies back and hums in some form of agreement. His skin is so creamy white. If I didn't know better, I'd think he's never seen the sun. Scars litter his stomach and thighs, but I don't draw attention to them. Instead, I finish undressing him, then lean down to tenderly kiss his now bare calf. Reid's breath hitches at the touch of my lips to his warm skin. I want to kiss him all over, bite him too, make him feel so good that he forgets about everything just for one night.

I kiss up his thighs, skip over his cock, and lick just below his belly button. His stomach goes concave as he gasps at the attention I'm lavishing on him. I lick and suck my way up his chest until I can finally lay claim to his mouth. Reid opens easily for me, our tongues entwining as I fuck mine into his mouth. He shivers underneath me when I dance my hands up his arms to grab his wrists, raising his arms until his fists press against my headboard.

"Grip the headboard bars," I whisper against his pliant mouth.

Reid immediately grips the headboard, no questions asked. I glance up to watch his fingers loop around the metal tight, holding on for dear life, knuckles popped and white.

"Like that?" Reid asks, voice oddly tentative.

"Just like that, baby." I press my forehead against his, watching as his eyes go distant as he tries to focus on me. "I'm gonna make you cry, but it might get scary. If you want to stop, let go of the headboard immediately. I'll stop, no questions asked, and give you whatever you need. Okay?"

Reid nods, his forehead moving against mine, but I need to hear the words or I can't do shit.

"Say it out loud, please."

"If I let go of the headboard, you'll stop," Reid says like the good boy he is.

I softly kiss the corner of his mouth. "Gonna fuck you this way so I can watch you cry, by the way."

Reid's breath stutters and a gorgeous flush works its way down his chest. God. I sit back on my haunches to survey Reid's body. He's fucking beautiful. I bend his legs toward his chest so I can pull his underwear off, keeping my eyes on his ass the entire time. I wonder how many smacks it would take for my handprint to glow red on his creamy skin. I lean over him one more time to kiss him, sweet and slow, until he's writhing underneath me trying to grind his cock against mine. I grab the lube before leaning back again, surveying Reid's body like I'm the king and his body is my kingdom. All laid out just for me.

I lube my finger up and press into him without any warning. Reid arches off the bed but remains quiet, not even a squeak rattles out of him. I fit myself between his splayed legs so that they fall over my thighs. The difference between his pale skin and my golden-tanned skin covered in tattoos only makes me more feverish. Our bodies are so different, but made to be like this together.

He's still tight after two fingers, but I think that's the way he'll like it. I grit my teeth as I coat my cock in lube because it feels too good. I need to be inside him. But before I do that, I want to taste him. Reid howls when I bend over to take his cock into my mouth. I pull off abruptly because he's not getting off that way, I just wanted a little taste.

Leaning over Reid, I firmly cover his mouth and nose with my hand and his eyes pop wide. He gasps against my hand as I push inside him. He's so fucking tight, Jesus. I remove my hand when I bottom out inside him, only to quickly replace it. He only got one good gasp in. Each time I pull out, I remove my hand for a brief second so he can breathe, then cover his mouth back up when I thrust back in. When his eyes start to roll back into his head, I yank my hand away and replace it with my mouth.

The kiss hurts. It's all teeth and biting and gnashing but it's the sexiest kiss of my life. Reid pours himself into every kiss with me, lets me own his mouth, make it mine. His body tenses under me, so I soften the kiss, slow my thrusts, until he's huffing in exasperation against my mouth.

"I was about to come," Reid whines, hands still tightly gripping the headboard.

"Not yet." I press my forehead to his sternum and grit my teeth.

Reid squawks in rage when I pull out. "Hey!"

"Let go of the headboard," I say roughly.

Reid immediately lets go of the headboard, arms hanging softly over his head. He looks the picture of an angel fallen from heaven like this, his platinum hair disheveled and damp with sweat. His light blue eyes are bright as he stares at me, cock still impossibly hard between his legs. I dive down on him, eagerly swallowing him to the back of my throat. When I shove two fingers inside him and peg his prostate, he curls over me, burying his fingers in my hair.

"Fuck! Dante!"

His thighs quiver as he tries to hold off his orgasm, so I suck him harder, needing to make him beg, make him hurt. He tenses again, so I pull off and hover over him. Reid's eyes are closed tight as his chest heaves. One more time.

I grab him by the hips and flip him over so that he's braced on his knees. His back is damp with sweat when I press against him, looming over him until he's shivering with need.

"Put your hands back on the headboard."

Reid's breath stutters. "Fuck."

His hands shake as he curls them back around the headboard. I nuzzle against his neck and kiss his ear. "How do you feel?"

"Green, but if you edge me one more time, it'll be yellow," Reid admits with a shake to his voice. Alright. No more edging.

I press against his hole, then thrust inside in one easy glide. Reid cries out and his fingers tighten enough on the headboard to make a few joints pop. This time I pound into him despite the building of my orgasm at the very base of my spine. I'm going to hold off until he comes if it's the last thing I do. I bury my hand in Reid's hair and yank his head to the side. His mouth is open as he pants, face flushed from desire, and a single tear slides down his cheek from the overstimulation. Fuck me.

Another tear slides loose when I thrust inside him so deep he might choke. My orgasm rips through me, rough and needy. Reid groans deep in his belly, his head going limp in my hold as he orgasms hands-free. The hottest thing I've ever seen. Fuck. Reid's fingers still grip the headboard tightly, so I lift my hand and rub his wrists until he lets go.

I stay inside him as I maneuver us onto our sides, curling behind him so he's nestled against me. Tangling our fingers together, I bring our joined hands to his chest. His heart is beating so fast I'm afraid it'll bust through his rib cage.

"Okay?" I whisper.

Reid snorts. "Shut up, you're ruining my high."

Fine. I bury my nose in his hair, letting the scent of his shampoo and cologne wash over me. When my cock softens enough to slip out, I gently roll Reid over to lie on his stomach. He goes easily, no ounce of fight remaining inside him. I stumble to the bathroom, wet a washcloth with warm water, then return to lovingly wipe him down. Reid lets out a little hiss of displeasure as I clean him up, but otherwise stays quiet.

I tug the blankets down on one side of the bed and slide him over so I can cover him up. He slits one eye open as I climb in beside him, tugging him until he's tucked against my chest.

"You did so good, Reid. You're perfect."

Reid shakes his head as much as he can as the sleep starts to consume him. "Not perfect. You'll get tired of me too. They all do."

My hand pauses at the top of his spine as I fight the urge to ask him what he means. He's loose and sleepy in my arms, beyond pliant, and it would be wrong to abuse that to get him to tell me things he never would any other time.

"I played in chess tournaments as a kid," I say, not knowing what else to do in this off-kilter moment.

Reid hums and snuggles closer. "I can see that. Did you wear glasses? I'd love that."

"No glasses," I deny, chuckling when Reid makes an aggrieved sound at the fact.

"I went to coding camp as a teen," Reid offers up.

"Me too."

Reid grunts against my chest, delightfully heavy, so perfectly mine at the moment. "In Pasadena?"

My fingers pause their gentle rubbing on the small of his back. Did we go to the same camp? There's no way. Life isn't *that* funny.

"Yeah, in Pasadena. I got a scholarship in my teens, something I didn't even apply for, and spent the two weeks at the camp. I've always been kind of a math whiz, but my family didn't understand it, so I spent more time on athletics to make it easier on them. I wonder if we were there the same year?"

"Hmm maybe. Funny."

"Yeah, funny."

"I loved being a kid. My parents were fun. Mason was *fun* then. Life used to be so much fun."

"And what is it now?" I press.

Reid sniffles. "Sad. I'm so alone."

"Not anymore, I'm here."

Reid snuggles somehow closer into me, like he wishes he could blend his small body with mine. I'd take him into my body if I could, to protect him, keep him safe. Something about Reid just feels like... mine.

"Need to brush my teeth," Reid mumbles, sounding delightfully sleepy.

"You can forget for one night."

"Parents paid a lot of money for braces," Reid says, already slumping heavily against me.

"It'll be okay for one night. Go to sleep."

Reid hums against my chest and snuggles closer. I sweep my hand over his back and nuzzle at the top of his head until he goes soft against me. His gentle snores lull me into sleeping as well. All my dreams are of Reid.

6

REID

W hen I finally blink awake, every muscle in my body aches like I've gone ten rounds in a boxing ring. The furnace at my back makes everything hurt just a touch less though. All those broken things inside of me shift around, like they're trying to fit back together without any glue. I wiggle deeper into Dante's arms since he's asleep and won't be able to judge my clinginess. After last night it's hard for me to rectify pulling away, fleeing his bedroom like I'd planned.

Dante's arm tightens around me in his sleep, as if he just can't help but hold me close. That's nice. But if I let him keep cuddling me, I'll fall back asleep, and with the way the sun is filtering through the curtains, it's definitely time for me to wake up. If I sleep too late, then I'll have absolutely no shot at sleeping tonight.

It takes me ten excruciating minutes to wiggle my way out of Dante's arms. When I roll out of bed, his arm instinctively reaches out to seek my warmth. I haphazardly shove a pillow toward him, which he cuddles against his chest with a pleased sigh. I will *not* find that cute.

After tugging on my underwear, I grab one of Dante's hoodies from a chair in the corner and slip it over my head. The house is eerily quiet as I tiptoe down the stairs. I assumed everyone was still asleep but one of Dante's roommates is standing at the stove making what appears to be French toast. The oven is also on and the room smells heavenly. My mouth instantly waters. I haven't eaten a real meal in days.

"Morning," the roommate calls without turning around. "I'm Jacob."

"Coffee?" I ask, voice still sleep rough.

Jacob nods to his left where a very fancy-looking coffee pot gurgles. I take one of the mugs already lined up beside it and fill it halfway, then root around in the fridge for creamer. Sugar's on the table, so I tip in a decent amount once I'm curled up in one of the wooden dining table chairs.

A timer goes off and I watch as Jacob bends over to take something out of the oven. Two things actually. He pulls out what looks like a quiche and flaky biscuits, plus fucking French toast. It's like a goddamn breakfast from a movie. Jacob slowly pours himself a cup of steaming coffee before joining me at the table. He's a good-looking guy. Dark brown hair, a couple of days' worth of scruff on his square jaw, and the kind of veiny forearms that make for very good art.

"So you're dating Dante?" Jacob asks nonchalantly.

I sputter around my sip of coffee. Jeez, warn a guy. "No. Not dating. Just... it's casual."

"Hmm." Jacob skewers me with a look that would make a weaker man squirm. "He's never had someone back at the house before. Usually just hookups at the club."

"Uhhh..."

"Just saying. He's dating you even if you aren't dating him."

"It's very nice of you to cook for your roommates," I say, desperately needing to change the topic before I lose my mind.

Jacob rolls his eyes affectionately. "If I didn't cook, Hayden would never eat."

"Oh... are you guys?"

Crimson paints Jacob's cheeks as he furiously shakes his head. "No, I would never date a roommate. We have too many entanglements. Plus Parker, he's my twin, he'd probably kill me for fucking with the *dynamic*." Jacob uses air quotes when he says "dynamic," which seems a little funny to me.

"Roommates date," I point out.

Jacob scoffs. "Sure, but not our kind of roommates."

That's weird. "Huh?"

Jacob shakes his head again, then climbs out of the chair, looking the very picture of a defeated man with slumped shoulders and an air of resignation. I stare transfixed as he dutifully fixes us both a plate of quiche with a biscuit on the side. I really want some of that damn French toast though. Quiet settles over us while we dig into the food which is mind-bogglingly delicious. My stomach doesn't know whether it should be pleased or outraged that I'm finally eating. Halfway through the meal, a sleepy Dante stumbles into the room. He grunts at Jacob while taking the empty seat beside me. Hooking his foot under my chair, Dante drags my chair closer until he can wrap his sleep-warm arm around my shoulders. The weight of him somehow instantly relaxes me, despite my lizard brain knowing it shouldn't.

Jacob disappears from the table and returns moments later with a mug of black coffee and a plate for Dante. I let

Dante keep his arm around me, his thumb gently sweeping over my bicep where his hand hangs. He seems to perk up after coffee and breakfast, but his eyes stay closed while he relaxes back into his chair. The two remaining roommates silently file into the room. I watch with curiosity as Jacob fixes two more plates and mugs of coffee. One of the other roommates appears to be Jacob's twin, the other is Hayden from the night before. Parker isn't as built like Jacob, a little wiry, but just as strong, his chin sharper. I wonder how many people think they're identical, but to me it's easy to see their differences. Hayden though, he's a Greek god if I've ever seen one. All golden-blond hair, tanned skin, and a smile that veers into terrifying with how unearthly it seems.

He is kind of weird though. Maybe even veering into creepy territory. All four boys have one thing in common; hotter than fucking sin. Parker and Jacob give off similar vibes to Dante, but not dangerous enough for me. I can tell underneath that veneer they're probably sweethearts. Whereas Hayden is just old-school hot. But it's the way Jacob looks at Hayden that captures my attention, especially when Hayden leans his chin against his propped-up hand and picks at the quiche.

"Don't like it?" Jacob asks haughtily.

"It's fine," Hayden mumbles.

"Consuming only sugar is bad for your brain."

Hayden spears Jacob with a thunderous sort of look. "I'm eating the damn eggs, aren't I?"

"It's too early for arguing," Parker mumbles around a biscuit. "Plus, we have company."

I lean further into Dante's embrace in hopes of going ignored. But Hayden's head sharply turns to sweep his gaze over me. He takes in my messy hair and Dante's hoodie hanging off of me. Dante protectively tightens his hold on me enough for Hayden to notice it.

"Morning, Reid," Hayden says with forced enthusiasm.

"Morning," I echo with my own pasted-on smile.

"Weird vibes." Parker leans across the table to steal the half-eaten biscuit off Hayden's plate. He tilts back in his chair, reaches into the cabinet, and pulls out a jar of Nutella. After smearing the biscuit with it, he plops it back on Hayden's plate. "There ya go, boss."

Hayden grins widely as he eats the biscuit. Jacob scowls first at Hayden, then at his twin, who just shrugs under the scrutiny. Everything gets more tense when Jacob stands, grabs the French toast I'd been eyeing, and promptly without further ado plops it in front of Hayden, who sends an absolutely disarming grim up at Jacob. Oh, that grin could melt *me*. Dante's obviously had enough of them because he clears our plates, then hurriedly hustles me back upstairs. Maybe he wants a second round before I go back home.

But Dante just closes his bedroom door, then backs me up against the hardwood to kiss me thoroughly. Oh. His fingers dig into my hips to tug me up higher, making it easier for him to lick into my mouth. Just as I'm about to offer to get on my knees, Dante abruptly pulls away with a pained groan.

"I've got too much homework to do today to be distracted by you," Dante mumbles before swooping back down to kiss me softly once more. This time his kiss lingers in a way that curls my toes against the cold hardwood floor. Yikes.

"I'll go." I shove him away and move around his room collecting my scattered clothing. I tug on my pants, but when I go to remove the hoodie, Dante stills me with a hand on my arm.

"Wear my hoodie home."

My nose instantly wrinkles. "Is this your way of marking me. Ugh, caveman."

Dante instantly flushes and urgently avoids my gaze. "No, it's just too cold outside for that damn leather jacket to be warm. I have enough hoodies to spare."

I hum but don't argue. I grab the aforementioned leather jacket from his desk, then head toward the door to leave.

"Reid?" Dante calls out.

I spin back around to face him. Dante wiggles his fingers for me to come closer, and the urge to say no is right on the tip of my tongue, but instead my body goes without a single ounce of fight. Dante kisses me again, then noses down my neck to my shoulder. Pain sluices through me when he bites down hard, surely hard enough to break skin. Dante wears a pleased-as-punch grin when he pulls away. That fucking—

"You always kiss me before you leave," Dante orders.

A shiver slips down my spine at his words. Pleased by catching me off guard, Dante spins me around with his big hands on my hips, and expertly guides me down the stairs. Almost as if he's done this before.

"Bye, Reid!" three voices simultaneously call out from the kitchen.

Dante's fingers tighten on my hips as he hurries me out the front door. Cold whips me in the face, but the sun is pleasantly warm. I expected Dante to point me in the direction of my house, then tell me to get to walking. But Dante only slings an arm over my shoulders and joins me on the short walk home. I can feel my face heat up from his proximity and his attention, but I also can't seem to make myself care.

"You've got class tomorrow morning, right?" Dante asks to

make conversation. I know he has my schedule memorized, just like I have his memorized.

"Yes."

"You want coffee? I'll meet you in the quad."

"Fine."

"So agreeable," Dante mumbles, then snorts. "I assume you want something that's more sugar and milk than coffee?"

"Mocha."

"Noted."

We stop in front of my house, Dante's arm still slung across my shoulders. He uses his arm to turn me toward him, pulling me into the warmth of his solid chest. The familiar scent of him washes over me and I close my eyes for one long second to memorize it. Dante doesn't look surprised when I push out of his embrace with an annoyed huff.

"Goodbye."

Dante's dark chuckle follows me into the house. I peek through the window to watch him head back home, a happy little pep to his step. I remove my shoes, gingerly placing them on the mat, before heading toward my room. The door to Mason's study is wide open as I walk by, so I pause to wave good morning.

Mason happily waves back. "You look perky."

I roll my eyes. "I had coffee."

"Just coffee?"

I flick him off and trudge the rest of the way to my room. I should take a shower, especially after the events of last night, but a part of me wants to keep the pieces of Dante that linger on my skin. The familiar smell of him lingers on the hoodie though, enough to quell my stupidest urges, so I guess I can take a shower. Once showered and delightfully clean, I tug the hoodie back over my head while my hair is still damp.

My phone lights up with a message from where it sits on the bed. I lean over slightly, tap the screen, and use all my willpower to stop from smiling at the sight of Dante's name. Motherfucker.

DANTE

> Be a good boy and draw me another picture.
> Give it to me tomorrow.

I IGNORE HIS TEXT.

The rest of the day is a blur of homework and sketching. Mason works on his computer on the couch, while I sit with my sketchbook nestled in my lap. When he's not looking, I sneak glances at him, noting the color in his cheeks, the vibrancy of his eyes.

Despite making his life as hellish as I can lately, I still worry about Mason more than I would any other sibling if I had one. I remember life before his illness when we were kids, and I remember how Mom hid him away from the world during and afterwards. One summer I got to go to coding camp, I took to it like I'd been made to do it. Poor Mason had wanted desperately to join me, but our mom had already been too far deep into "protecting Mason" mode. No, too many germs, she'd sang. Enough germs for me, but too many for Mason. I'd come home every night when I was twelve and showed an almost-ready-for-college Mason how to code. It'd been our secret that summer, one of many that we'll probably always have.

Ever since our parents died, there's been this divide

between us that I somehow just can't cross. I want to hug him, but he won't let me, because he physically can't allow it. And I want to tell him I'm sorry for always being such a little shit but the ability to apologize for any of my behavior is simply impossible now.

Mason yawns around bed time after spending hours typing nonstop. He looks over at me, but I purposefully hide my face so it looks like I've been sketching for hours, not staring at him while going all maudlin. He leaves the living room with a sigh, and my heart hurts so much that I don't know what to do with it.

Once the sounds of Mason getting ready for bed quiet, I make my way to my own room, snuggling down into the bed still dressed in Dante's hoodie. Lifting it to my nose, I take a deep inhale, calming at the spicy scent of his cologne and skin. And if my heart beats just a little faster when I fall asleep that night, well, that's between me and God.

————

I WAKE up early the next morning to spend time in the library. Sometimes getting out of the house helps me focus on a task at hand. The sun hangs low in the sky, campus quiet as I make my way toward the library. Usually I'd have coffee in my hand to keep me warm, but I don't want to drink any since Dante will be bringing me some later.

That feeling of being watched niggles at the back of my brain again, but I assume it's just Dante. A smile tugs at my lips, making me dip my head down to hide the blush that's no doubt working its way up my neck. Libraries have the most amazing, comforting smell. Old books and magic, that's what my mother used to say before taking me and Mason to the library as children. Something about a library just settles my nerves, makes me feel like maybe everything is going to be alright. Even when Mason was sick as a kid, we'd find our way to the library, and nothing could hurt us there when we escaped into another world.

The library is almost empty when I push through, everyone my age still asleep. Just the way I like it. I head up to the third floor where the research texts are and navigate my way through the empty oak tables. My usual one is empty, with the deep scratches in the corner from someone practicing their whittling skills as they studied.

I drag my sketchbook out of my bag, along with my laptop and textbook. An hour of studying at the library before class will give me enough time to work ahead so that I can finish the course materials before finals season occurs. I usually like to jump ahead in my courses, because I often already know what they're teaching.

By the beginning of high school, I was taking college-level courses. A college senior at nineteen would've thrilled my parents, too bad they're not around to see it. I scowl at my train of thought and focus back on my work. When the numbers start to annoy me because they're too predictable, I grab my sketchbook to doodle a distraction. That feeling of being watched again washes over me.

When I glance up, movement behind some books catches my eye. The familiar shine of Dante's hair is easy to spot. I smile down at the sketchbook again, then reach into the pocket of my hoodie to grab my phone.

When do I get my coffee?

DANTE

When you're good

What do I have to do to be good?

DANTE

Take your cock out

MY CHEST HEAVES as I stare down at those words. Is he serious? I think about arguing with him, telling him to fuck off, but I also think about that glorious feeling of pleasing him from a few nights ago. Pleasing Dante has quickly become one of my favorite pastimes. I clear my throat awkwardly as I slip my hand under the desk, unbuttoning my pants with one hand.

DANTE

Keep your other hand on the table, flat.

I DO AS he says with a stutter in my breath.

DANTE

Good boy. Now take your cock out.

MY COCK IS ALREADY ROCK HARD, pre-cum leaking from the tip when I swipe my thumb over the head. A hushed sound reaches my ears despite the blood pounding in my head.

DANTE

Now make yourself come

You have five minutes

I KEEP my eyes trained on the scratch marks at the edge of the table as I shuttle my hand over my cock. It's dry and not the most pleasurable jerk-off experience of my life, but the idea of doing it in public, with Dante watching in the wings, makes it somehow the top ten best masturbation sessions of my life. My balls tighten and the base of my spine tingles as my orgasm creeps up on me. I gasp quietly and tilt my head more, ducking my chin into the hoodie that still smells like Dante.

Spilling into my hand, I close my eyes tight as my orgasm washes over me. I pant softly through my release, not at all shocked when Dante's warm body presses against my back.

"Give me your hand," Dante mutters into my ear.

My face must be beet red when I lift my cum-covered hand from under the table. Dante presses his cheek against my own, lifts my hand to his mouth, and licks my cum from my hand. Oh fuck. If anyone saw us, it would look totally depraved. Because it is. We're both sick.

"It's time to go to class now."

Dante's heat disappears from my back before I can even try to kiss him. After shakily buttoning my pants back up, I pack my things away, and trudge out of the library. I can feel Dante's eyes on me, his presence close by as I walk across the street to the math building.

All through class my body thrums from the release in the library. I wish I could've fallen to my knees and sucked Dante off there, eyes staring up at him in proof of being a good boy. Only his good boy. I want everyone to see just how good I can be for him. By the time class is over, I feel like I'm in some sort of trance where all I can think about is Dante.

Dante stands at the edge of the quad when I exit the math building. The sunlight makes his dark hair look like onyx, like coal. My fingers itch to draw him like he is right now, broad-shouldered, annoyed curl of his lips until he catches sight of me. The transformation of his face from annoyed to delighted should be illegal. I should not have that effect on anyone, let alone someone as glorious as Dante.

"Mocha," Dante announces while holding a cup out to me.

I take it with the most bland look I can muster. "Thank you."

Dante glances over my shoulder with a frown, then slings his arm over my shoulder. "How was class?"

I glance over my shoulder, but don't see anything. Odd. I let him lead me deeper into the quad where a couple of other people are lounging around on the grass. He plops down on the ground without any fanfare and opens his arms. When I just stare down at him in confusion, he wiggles his fingers in a clear sign for me to join him. Sighing, I sit between his legs with my back to his chest.

"Class was fine," I mumble while taking a sip of the coffee.

"You're a math major?"

I hum in agreement. "I want to be an accountant."

Dante's hand stills in its petting of my arm. "Seriously? I wouldn't have pegged you for that."

"I want to be a forensic accountant. I like solving puzzles."

"Makes a little more sense now," Dante murmurs before tucking his head into the crook of my neck. He noses around for a second before placing a kiss at the spot he bit yesterday morning. A zip of electricity shoots down my spine at the touch of his lips to the bite. "Hayden says you're very smart. He doesn't say that about people a lot considering he's some certified genius type shit."

"Oh?"

Dante nods against my neck. "He's getting some degree in math so he can work on going to space."

"Interesting. And you?"

"Me what?" Dante asks in clear confusion.

I angle my head to look him in the eyes. "What's your major?"

"Oh," Dante says in surprise. He looks sheepish for a moment, then shrugs. "Engineering."

"Right." I knew that already, just wanted him to say it. "And what do you want to be when you grow up?"

"Structural engineer. Building bridges and tunnels."

"That's cute."

Dante's eyebrows lift into his hairline. "Cute?"

I nod while taking a slow sip of my coffee. Warmth spreads through me when Dante tracks my tongue swipe over my lip. For a moment I think he's going to dip down and kiss me, but his gaze once again pings to the other side of the quad.

"Okay, why do you keep looking over there?" I attempt to

turn my head to look, but Dante's fingers on my chin stop me. "What the fuck?"

"Keep your eyes on me. Laugh, now."

I laugh awkwardly. "What is going on?"

Dante smiles, but it's not his real smile. This smile is terrifying and fake. The type of smile an alien would give when attempting to learn how to be human.

"We're going to get up and walk back to my house, okay? Don't argue with me. Just trust me, alright?"

Every single molecule in my body screams at me to argue. But the firmness of Dante's direction, the slightly frantic look in his eyes easily convinces me to keep quiet. So, I listen. We slowly stand and Dante carefully removes my backpack to sling it over his shoulder. When he takes my hand in his, it feels less like it did the other night, and more like he wants to ensure there's no way for me to be taken away. His grip is so tight my fingers ache.

Fear washes through me, because Dante doesn't seem the type to be worried. Doesn't seem the type to run away. Dante is danger incarnate, so what in the world could ever spook him? The walk to his house feels like the shortest yet longest walk of my life. Probably because Dante is unusually quiet.

When we step inside, Dante grabs me by the shoulders and shakes me a little. "There is *so* much I have to tell you, but you are about to get a crash course in some very serious information, so just stay super chill. Okay?"

"I... what?"

Dante shakes his head. "There's not enough time. Come on."

He drags me into the living room where the three other boys are already waiting. Their eyes snap to me, then immediately snap back to Dante. Dante roughly manhandles me into one of the wingback chairs situated in the corner away from the window. Scully meows from the ground and jumps into my lap, causing shocked gasps to rattle through the boys. I pet between her ears, letting the softness of her black fur calm me. A rumble of a purr escapes her and I smile, despite the harrowing situation I seem to currently be in. Who doesn't love a purring cat in their lap?

Dante steps over to the window and peeks out of the corner of the blinds. His fingers go straight, then flex as if he's fighting the urge to punch something.

"There's a tail on Reid," Dante announces like that should mean something to me.

Three gazes immediately ping to me.

"Why is there a tail on Reid?" Parker asks with a furrow between his brows.

Dante shrugs. "I noticed it this morning. He followed Reid to the math building, waited outside, then followed us into the quad."

Indignation rolls through me. "You were watching me *still*? After the library?"

Dante once again looks unrepentant. "I never said I was going to stop. And don't even try to say a word because I know you *still* follow me."

"This sounds like foreplay," Jacob interrupts with an odd little smirk.

"Shut up," Dante and I say simultaneously.

Dante's hard gaze lands back on me. "Why do you have a tail?"

"How the fuck would I know? I go to class, go home. I don't go to clubs anymore. I don't have hookups. I haven't done anything!"

"Maybe it's because of you," Hayden accuses, gaze firmly on Dante.

"Me?" Dante asks, clearly affronted.

Hayden stands from the couch and joins Dante by the window. He stares out the blinds for a moment, fingers anxiously tapping against his thighs. I watch on like a distant observer. This all might be about me, but why are they all so shaken?

Parker stands from the sofa, ignored by everyone else in the room. He nods toward the kitchen in a clear signal for me to follow. But I'm not sure I'm allowed to move. Dante plopped me down here for a reason. Parker sighs loudly when I don't immediately follow.

"Reid, come to the kitchen with me."

Dante's head turns toward Parker, then his gaze swings toward me. He nods in permission, so I stand and slowly follow Parker to the kitchen. Scully plods along behind us as if she wants to be privy to our conversation as well. Sweet little thing.

Parker pours two mugs of coffee, then stands on his tiptoes to reach into a cabinet. A bottle of expensive whiskey is in his hand when he lowers back down. I swallow loudly as he pours generous amounts of liquor into both cups, then hands one of them to me.

I take a sip and grimace, it tastes more like whiskey than coffee. But I guess the occasion calls for it.

"Your brother, what does he do?" Parker asks, mug held to his lips.

I narrow my eyes. "How do you know about my brother?"

Parker grins. "I've got my ways. I probably know you better than Dante. I have to ensure anyone that one of my brothers is bringing into the circle isn't a total waste of space.

I deem you worthy, but your brother is a crack in the armor. Tell me, do you know what he does for work?"

"He..." I pause because I really don't know.

Parker hums. "I couldn't find it anywhere either. Found a lot on you, but not much on Mason. I know he became your legal guardian when your parents died."

I gasp. "Who the fuck are you people?"

Of course that's when Dante decides to swagger into the kitchen. Dante looks between Parker and me, clearly taking in how both of us have our hackles raised. Parker lifts his hands in defense, promptly fleeing the kitchen before Dante can lay into him. I expect Dante to talk me down, do something to help me understand what's going on, but all he does is tangle our fingers together and guide me back to the living room. Hastily, I gulp down the coffee in hopes it'll steady my nerves.

"Okay, so you know Robin Hood, right?" Dante asks as he shoves me back down in the chair.

"Sure..."

He sweeps his hand toward himself and the guys on the couch. "Meet your modern-day Robin Hoods."

7

DANTE

R eid stares blankly up at me. One second, two seconds, then his eyes narrow in the way that I know means I'm about to get some serious shit.

"Explain," Reid says, voice carrying a hint of anger.

"We were recruited by someone we've never met to steal back what's been stolen from the people. Sometimes it's money, sometimes it's intellectual property... sometimes we kill people." I pause and blink down at Reid, waiting for him to catch on. "Do you understand what I'm saying?"

Reid takes a deep breath. "Are you fucking with me?"

"Nope!" Hayden pipes up from the sofa. "We were all recruited. We've been doing this for about three years now."

"Are you paid?"

"We have a stipend," I explain, desperately needing him to understand. "But we aren't really paid as much as you'd think. It's more... something we all want to do. The rent on the house is kindly paid for us by our benefactor."

"You avenge people for... basically free?" Reid asks in

disbelief, mouth adorably pursed. If this situation wasn't so precarious, I'd do something insane like try to cuddle him.

"We have our reasons," Jacob calls from the couch.

Reid's eyes slowly track over everyone in the room. "You kill people?"

"Bad people," Jacob corrects, but flinches when it clearly doesn't appease Reid.

"Excuse me," Reid says, then slowly stands. He pauses for a moment to look over everyone one last time, before leaving the room. For one awful moment I'm afraid he's going to leave, but he only climbs up the stairs, shoulders up to his ears, back ramrod straight.

"Oh... you're in trouble," Jacob sings.

Parker shoots his twin a glare. "You're one to talk."

"What?" Jacob asks in confusion.

Okay, maybe Parker isn't as oblivious as I thought. Jacob definitely is though. I leave them be and climb the stairs two at a time to my room, too fucking eager to get to Reid. He's standing in the middle of my room, arms wrapped tightly around himself, gazing listlessly at the floor. When I close the door and lean against it, Reid's hard gaze bores into mine.

"Was it all a lie?" Reid asks quietly.

Now I'm confused. "What?"

"Am I a mark?"

Oh no. I rush toward him but Reid takes a careful step back. I fall to my knees before him.

"No, Reid. You've never been a mark, not to me. You've only ever been mine. Just mine. Okay? Please believe me... I'll do anything. I'll give you *anything*."

Reid's blue eyes pierce through me. Bruised light blue carnations, that's the color of his eyes. So much fucking pain and anger, half directed at me, half directed at himself.

Fucking Reid. The fact that even for a second he thought... thought that he isn't everything to me after just a few weeks. Fuck. How do I make him understand? His jaw clenches hard as he turns his head away from me. All emotion disappears from his face, even the sadness. I can feel it, the moment he shuts down.

"Reid, don't do this." I reach out and pull at his hoodie, tugging him slightly closer to me. "Look at me."

Reid's distant gaze falls back on me. "Why do you want me?"

"'Cause you're mine."

He yanks out of my grasp and tries to skirt past me, but I'm not allowing it. I roll to my feet and grab him around the waist, easily tossing him onto the bed. Reid flails in anger, fists curled tight, but I don't give a shit. I fit myself between his thighs, forcing them to splay around my waist. Reid thrashes and kicks to break free, but I grab his wrists to hold them over his head.

"Stop it," I order, voice firm and low.

Reid stops thrashing but looks up at me with all the power of a thousand angry burning suns. This is the way I like him, all fight and fury, because it makes it so earned when he melts into a mellow puddle of want just for me.

"You're more annoyed that you might've been a mark than the fact I kill people. Absolutely amazing."

"You kill *bad* people," Reid says through his teeth, clearly mocking me.

"Yeah, that's right, baby. I steal from the rich, from the assholes, and give it back to the rightful owners. Sometimes that means I kill people that deserve it. Am I fucked up? Probably. But you're just as fucked up as me. Now what do you need? Need me to make you cry?"

Reid's glare would bring weaker men to ruin. But I like when he fights back and I like when he lets me show him who's actually in charge here. Because it's him. He *allows* me to be in charge because he wants it, because he enjoys it. That's the real power exchange between us.

His silence tells me more than words ever could. Reid surges up to kiss me, teeth biting my lip so hard he draws blood. I swear and lift my other hand to his throat, pressing hard enough to make him gasp against my mouth.

"I'm not letting you come," I say against his mouth.

Reid cries out when I firmly press my cock against his hip. His fingers flex and claw at my hands, but I hold on, uncaring. I rise up onto my knees, then slowly lift each one until I'm straddling his stomach. Shoving his shirt up under his arms, I use my one free hand to unbutton my jeans and push them down. Reid hisses when I slip my cock out, already hard and leaking just from a few seconds of manhandling him.

"Lick." I lift my hand to his mouth and he immediately obeys. "Good boy."

Reid's eyes immediately go glassy at the praise. He thinks it's danger he wants, to feel something, but that's not it at all. Reid needs me to tell him he's good while simultaneously making him feel like he's bad. I lean over him while working my cock over. His breath fans across my face with each ragged breath. His hands flex in my grasp again, but I hold steady. I wish I was inside him again, pressing his face into the mattress until he can't even attempt to breathe.

I kiss him again, moaning into his mouth when he shakes underneath me. Maybe it's desire, maybe it's fear, I don't know anymore. Calling it desire is so much easier. The head of my cock rubs against his stomach with each snap of my hips into my hand, driving my need higher until my toes curl against the bed. Reid's eyes go from glassy and distanced, to sharp and needy. I've got him right where I want him.

He leans up slightly to take my mouth in a kiss, different from the last one. This kiss is soft, at war with the fast shuttling of my hand over my cock. I need to come. Reid moans into my mouth again, all want and need, and it shocks the orgasm out of me. I yank away from him to sit up on my knees, then spread my cum all over his stomach, painting him as mine.

"You're mine, don't you fucking forget it."

Reid stares up at me with a mix of anger and all sharp edges. But I wasn't lying when I said he couldn't come. I won't let him. Not now. I tug his sweater down, then lean down to place a gentle, close-mouthed kiss against his still parted lips.

"Now can we go back downstairs to figure this shit out?"

Reid tiredly closes his eyes. "Is my brother safe?"

"We'll see. But right now my priority is you. Nobody will touch you while you're mine."

Reid lets me lift him out of the bed, even lets me wrap an arm around him as I guide him to the bathroom. I wash my hands, then use a washcloth to wipe the corners of his eyes, and his cheeks. He stares up at me the entire time, face still carefully devoid of emotion. It scares me a little bit, how easily he can make himself a blank canvas.

"You okay?" I ask softly.

Reid blinks rapidly a few times as if rebooting back online. His gaze slowly focuses on me, but instead of replying with words, he tips up on his toes and soundly kisses me. I keep my eyes open and so does Reid. Somehow that's more intimate than both of us closing our eyes. The kiss is just barely a brush of lips, but when he pulls away, his lips tip up slightly at the corners in the approximation of a pleased smile.

"I'm okay now."

"Yeah?"

Reid blows out a long breath. "Yeah, yeah I'm okay. I really need a cigarette though since you didn't let me come."

"No smoking inside," I say firmly. "Also, you shouldn't be smoking at all."

Reid rolls his eyes, but there's an underlying hint of affection that was never there before. "Let a man have some vices."

"You like to be choked to an inch of death, that's a big enough vice."

Reid flushes bright red, but doesn't reply. I love the way his flushes paint his creamy cheeks, it works all the way down his neck to his chest, and it's so easy to read him when it happens. I tangle our fingers together and tug Reid behind me back to the living room. The guys are still sitting on the couch, but now Jacob and Hayden are playing video games while Parker silently reads a well-worn hardcover in the corner.

Parker looks up first, eyebrows raised. "Can we continue now?"

"Yes, I had to sort... something out. All sorted."

Parker's eyes flick between me and Reid, but he stays quiet because he's not a total idiot. Like Jacob.

"We heard everything, you know," Jacob teases.

"Oh yeah?" Reid asks as he tosses himself in the chair. "What'd you hear?"

"Lots of moaning and *oh yeah*s," Hayden chimes in.

Reid snorts. "You didn't hear shit. Dante is a quiet fuck."

Jacob's eyebrows go up. "That's way more information than I ever needed to know about him."

"You started it," Reid teases with a wicked smirk.

I sit on the edge of the chair beside him. His arm brushes against my thigh when he leans a little closer, but I don't draw attention to it. I have to take the small wins when I can. Now I have to deal with the matter at hand.

"They're probably tracking Reid because they saw me trailing him. Maybe they think he's... worth something to us. Not in the way they think," I say when Reid's eyebrows rise. "He probably needs twenty-four-seven protection until we can figure this shit out. We've righted a lot of wrongs, these people could be *anyone.*"

"Move him in here, then, because I'm not having us all switch on and off to keep him safe outside the house," Hayden orders without taking his gaze off of the television. "I'm in some of his classes, so he's safe there. He'll just need to be watched when he's going to and from campus. One of us should probably drive him."

Reid groans. "Drive to campus? It'll take longer than walking."

Hayden shrugs, totally uncaring. "Die, then."

Parker sighs loudly and Jacob angrily pinches his nose. That's so very Hayden. Point-blank and take it or leave it. The method seems to work on Reid because his jaw tightens, but he doesn't argue.

"I'll take you to your house so you can get a few things, okay?" I tell him.

Reid nods once, then looks down at his bitten-down nails.

"Has anyone informed Robin yet?" Parker asks, because he's always the one thinking ahead.

When all he receives is silence, Parker sighs again and pulls out his phone. He types a quick message, then waves his hand at the three of us. Our phones all vibrate at the same time to alert us of an incoming message with us attached. I've got to assume they'll help handle this situation for a while so I can focus on Reid. This is exactly why I don't date, because while what we do isn't *bad,* it's inherently dangerous since we're fucking with people that don't typically get fucked with.

"We'll be right back." I hurriedly drag Reid out of the chair and out the front door. Slinging my arm around his shoulder, I keep a careful eye out for the man I noticed earlier. He's there, a hundred or so feet back, but he's easy to spot when I've spent the last few years keeping an eye out for people exactly like him.

"Is he there?" Reid whispers.

"Yeah, but I've got you."

Reid lifts his hand to twine his fingers with mine at his shoulder. At any other time I'd find the move adorably cute, but I recognize it for what it is now. Reid's anxious as hell, his eyes crinkled at the corners in concentration. I follow Reid into his house, carefully toeing my shoes off like last time.

"Reid?" Mason calls out from the kitchen.

Mason wears a soft smile when he spots his brother, but his eyes turn curious when he sees me trailing slowly behind. I lift my hand in a shy wave.

"What's going on?" Mason asks, clearly worried.

Reid awkwardly clears his throat. "I'm going to stay with Dante for a few days. Nothing big. Will you be in town? Or do you have a business trip?"

"I... No, I'm staying here. What's going on?" Mason repeats, an edge of hysteria creeping into his voice.

Reid steps forward and goes to touch Mason, but hurriedly retracts his hands as if burned. I watch as Reid stuffs his hands into his pockets, eyebrows furrowed as he stares Mason down.

"I just need to get away for a few days. We might take a trip to the mountains, get away. Okay?"

"Alright," Mason says softly. "You're okay?"

Reid smiles, but it's clearly fake. At least to me. "I'm fine. The best I've been in months. I'll text you."

I follow behind Reid up the stairs. He immediately shoves a bag into my arms with a strongly muttered curse. Reid packs in a flurry of movement, seemingly grabbing things at random, but I'm sure there's a method to his madness. It's disconcerting how little he packs before telling me he's ready to go.

"That's it?" I ask in disbelief.

Reid holds up his hand and ticks one finger down. "I sleep naked." He ticks another finger down. "My backpack is already at your house." He ticks another down. "There's food for me there." And he puts his thumb down so that only his middle finger is left up. "I'm not staying there forever, I'm coming back home."

"Maybe I'll keep you forever," I say before crashing our mouths together.

"Hey!" Reid squawks against my mouth, but that just makes it easier for me to kiss him. Once he's still in my arms, I pull away to stare down at him in awe. A perfect creature.

"This means you have to do what I say because I'm ordering you around to keep you alive."

Reid snorts. He punches me in the stomach hard. "Get bent."

The grin on my face burns as I stare after him. When I

finally descend the stairs with his bag in hand, I find Reid standing close enough to Mason to almost touch. Now that they're so close, I can see the similarities. If Reid had his natural hair color, they could almost be twins. The same gentle slope to their nose, heart-shaped face, and cheekbones that could cut glass.

Reid reaches up to tap his nose three times, making me tilt my head. Mason smiles softly and lifts his hand up to repeat the tapping on his own nose. They both smile at each other, before Reid stomps out of the kitchen and toward the front door. I wave at Mason again before fleeing after Reid so he doesn't get himself stolen in broad daylight.

"What was with the tapping thing?" I ask.

Reid stomps faster so that I have to jog slightly to keep up. He might be shorter than me but damn he can walk fast. What the hell.

"It's how we say goodbye," Reid says with a little too much forced cheer. He's lying.

"Okay."

"Okay," Reid repeats.

"Does he need someone to watch him? Do you want that?"

Reid's eyes twitch again. "If it's possible, I'd like someone to watch over him. If something happens to him because of me or you, I'll never forgive myself."

"Done."

Reid pauses on the sidewalk, making me have to slide to a stop to turn back. "It's that easy?"

"Yeah, whatever you want," I quickly agree.

Tilting his head, he gives me that predator look again, the one that always unsettles me just a little. Reid sniffs, lifts his chin in the air, then continues on back toward my house. We walk the rest of the way in comfortable silence. The guys aren't in the living room and the house is quiet, but I don't have the patience to worry about them right now. Reid heads up toward my room like he lives there. Now he does. The caveman inside me practically preens at this turn of events.

I set his bag down on the desk in the corner of my room. When I turn around, Reid is toeing off his boots again. Without a care in the world, he tosses himself on the bed to stare up at the ceiling. I lie down beside him, cheek against the pillow, hand on the comforter between us. My breath catches in my chest as I wait for him to turn on the bed, and when he does I have to bite back a smile.

Reid narrows his eyes at me and tangles our fingers together. "Why do you do that? Why do you bite back your smile?"

"My smile is creepy."

Reid tuts. "Not your genuine smile. Your fake one yeah, it's a little... serial killer. But the real smile when something makes you happy? That's golden. Do it more, please."

"Okay, but... don't tell anyone."

Reid rolls his eyes. "I'll send it out in my next mass email."

"No, you won't."

He sighs and rolls over to cuddle against my chest. "No, I won't."

Reid falls asleep for a little nap, but I'm wide awake. I listen to him breathe for a while, run my fingers through his hair, play with his fingers that are curled softly against the comforter. Watching Reid has quickly become my only obsession. Since that first time I laid eyes on him in the club, it's felt like he's mine. Insanity, sure, but it doesn't make it any less true. I'll do anything to keep him safe. Anything.

The door opens slowly, only for Hayden to peek his head through.

"Jacob said dinner is ready," Hayden says with a teasing smirk.

"Could text me that."

"I'm nosy."

Hayden closes the door with a little slam, startling Reid awake. He rolls onto his back with a groan and blinks wide eyes up at me. I smile down at him and he tentatively smiles back.

"See, pretty," Reid says softly.

I kiss him until his stomach is grumbling. Downstairs smells like stew and bread, Jacob's favorite comfort meal to cook for us. Reid keeps his fingers knotted with mine even as we take our respective seats. Parker and Hayden join us just as Jacob is setting a pot of steaming stew in the middle of the table. Jacob smacks the back of Parker's head in some sort of twin signal. The next minute Parker is scrambling out of his seat to help set the table while Jacob brings freshly baked bread over to the table.

"Is this what it's like every night?" Reid asks around a mouthful of biscuit.

I give him a hesitant smile. "Most nights."

Reid hums thoughtfully, then gently bumps his shoulder into mine. "It's nice."

Yeah, yeah it is. Nicer now that he's here. But I'll bite my tongue on that one for a bit. We eat dinner quietly, which is par for the course for us. If we aren't sniping at one another, usually we're silent, either in our own heads, working on something for Robin, or doing homework. Once we're done with dinner, I leave Reid at the table while I help Parker do the dishes. I rinse them, then Parker loads them into the dishwasher.

"You really trust him to tell him all that," Parker murmurs just after sneaking a look over his shoulder to confirm Reid is occupied.

"We've imprinted on one another."

Parker grunts so loudly that Hayden turns a suspicious eye on us. I make a face and Hayden turns away, so I go back to washing dishes.

"You do have that sort of energy. It's like... you'll take anyone... but when the important person comes along, BAM they're yours."

"Yes, imprinting."

"Dante, where did you learn that word?" Parker asks in only the way he can. He's not saying I'm stupid, he's just fucking curious.

"Those vampire movies."

Parker shakes his head ruefully. "Absolutely astounding. I'd kill for you, Dante."

"Obviously."

"I wonder how he would do with a gun?"

My insides shrivel up and die at the idea of Reid with a gun. "No gun for him. Maybe a taser."

Parker stares at me with a look of total disgust, before he shakes his head free of it and continues to load the dishwasher until we're all done. Reid having a gun is a huge no-go for me. I don't even like carrying a gun. Over my dead body am I letting spitfire Reid handle a gun. We'd be on the local news in ten seconds flat. But a taser? Yeah, I'm fine with that. He can tase someone's balls off for all I care. Although there is that saying if you're willing to handle a taser, you've got to be tased. The idea of Reid being tased is almost just as bad as him handling a gun. Jesus fucking Christ, I need to put him in a bubble.

Once we're done with the dishes, we turn around to find the kitchen empty. The sound of video games comes from the living room, so Parker and I amble our way there. Reid sits comfortably in the corner of the couch. He looks so much like he was meant to be there that my heart hurts a little with the force of it. I've felt alone even while with these boys for so long, that having Reid there balances it all out.

Reid sticks his tongue out and wrinkles his nose, making me bite back a grin. It's a little painful to bite my cheeks to contain my obvious like for him, but better that than endure any sort of hassling or teasing from the guys. I join Reid on the couch, slinging my arm around his thin shoulders. He leans heavily into my side, either on purpose, or just out of habit by now, but I don't care either way as long as he leans against me.

"Can I ask questions? I have a lot of questions," Reid says into the room.

Parker raises one eyebrow from his spot on the couch, while Jacob and Hayden simultaneously turn to stare at Parker.

"Low-key forgot you were here," Jacob admits, mouth tilting up at one corner. Little shit.

"You can ask whatever you want," Hayden says and returns his attention to the television.

"Well.... Why did Robin pick all of you?" Reid asks first.

Jacob points at Parker.

Parker sighs.

Hayden laughs.

I turn my head to nuzzle my nose into Reid's sweet-smelling hair. Cotton candy, that's what his hair smells like.

"We don't really know why... we just got checks in the mail with a timestamp to a location. Neither of us could turn it down after what we were offered... and I've always had a penchant for firearms, so it worked out." Parker leans forward on his elbows, eyes gleaming. "Over the years we've gleaned a few things though. Dante was recruited for his brawn and protective nature. He's a grumpy shit but he'd lay down his life without thought for someone he loves. I was recruited for my attention to detail, probably helps that I've gotten straight As literally my entire life without much trying. Jacob was recruited because he's my brother." Jacob snorts at that because it's decidedly wrong, but we all let Parker get away with it. "And Hayden was recruited because the team needed a blond."

Hayden laughs in delight, but doesn't tear his gaze from the video game.

"That sounds fake," Reid replies.

Parker shrugs nonplussed. "Hayden's also a certified genius that skates under the radar because he looks like he should be hazing someone at a fraternity instead of hacking into a fortune 500 company and fleecing some CEOs for all they're worth."

"That is true," Jacob agrees.

A red flush steals over Hayden's cheeks but his jaw just tightens, and he locks in harder in hopes of defeating the boss they've been working toward in the video game they're playing. Nothing makes Hayden blush like a compliment from Jacob. Scully pads down the stairs, tail up in the air, and chin high as she looks over the scene before her. Typically she pads right to Hayden, curls up in his lap, and stays there happily for hours. But much to Hayden's chagrin, Scully swaggers across the living room and plops herself down on Reid's lap.

I don't dare move to break whatever spell Scully is under. This is her house and we all just live here. But Reid doesn't get the big deal, I guess, because he just rests his hand on her back and pets her like she's any normal cat. Maybe she only has a thing for blonds.

"Well, what happened after you were recruited? You all didn't just... become this way overnight." Reid huffs a little when I place a gentle kiss behind his ear, loving the softness of his skin there. "Cut it out," Reid implores, but his tone is empty, so I keep placing kisses to the sensitive skin of his ear as the boys continue our story.

"No, we went through a few months of training before our first mission," Parker says with his gaze back on the book in his lap. His tone is idle and bored, how he often gets when detaching from a moment with us. "A private kickboxing gym, hand-to-hand combat, firearms training at a gun range in the next town over. We all had some hacking skills too, but we have our specialties, which is why Hayden is the prince among us. He knows *all* coding because his brain does something once and absorbs it like cereal absorbs milk."

"Cute analogy," Hayden calls out, obviously pleased.

"Thank you, I liked it as well," Parker replies with a grin in his voice.

"So when do we get to ask you questions?" Hayden asks, swearing while jamming the buttons on the controller. Jacob also starts to swear and suddenly the room is filled with them yelling at the screen. Video games have never been my thing, but sometimes it's fun to watch them get all riled up. One would think they'd fight against each other in the games, but they always team up, then snipe at each other the entire time. Always a lively experience.

Reid turns his head to glare at me after one well-placed kiss. "I'm an open book."

I skim my fingers down his arm, watching as goose pimples pop across his skin, but he holds himself steady to make himself appear unaffected by my touch. Even without opening his mouth he's trying to lie to me.

"Why aren't you running away? You're in a room full of murderers and you just want to know how we got trained?" Jacob asks, flicking a look over his shoulder at Reid and me all cuddled up on the couch. I flick him off and his gaze returns to the screen.

"I have a thing for danger," Reid retorts, tone sarcastic, but only I know the truth.

Yeah, he has a thing for danger. But when he says that, he means *me*.

8

REID

I don't know why I pegged Dante as a cuddler. He's definitely not though. I wake up in a rush like usual, jarred awake by my body's inability to sleep past six in the morning. When I roll over onto my side, it's to find Dante starfished out on his stomach, one arm under a pillow, the other reaching out toward me, his fingertip just barely grazing my bicep. His head is angled away from me, his dark hair messy from no doubt tossing and turning all night.

He's kind of adorable.

Even the thought pisses me off.

Rubbing the sleep from my eyes, I sigh quietly to avoid waking Dante up. How did I get myself into this situation? I went from aimless club twink to suddenly intertwined with a group of vigilantes. Now, because I'm mixed up with them, there's a bullseye on my back. As if sensing my thoughts, Dante turns his head, blinks one sleepy eye at me, then groans loudly.

"What the fuck? It's still dark out." Dante grabs my arm and yanks until he can manhandle me into his arms. I squawk and try to wiggle free, but his arm is a tight band around my body. "You're not going anywhere. Stop it."

"I'm not a prisoner."

Dante chuckles darkly. "You kind of are. At least until we can figure out what they want with you."

"Isn't it obvious?" I ask, voice dripping with sarcasm.

"Oh?" Dante says innocently.

"It's because I'm with you. They'll get to you through me blah blah blah. Don't you watch action movies?"

Dante places a soft kiss to the nape of my neck, making a shiver work its way down my spine. I attempt to hide my body's reaction, but Dante's knowing upturned lips press against my skin.

"I don't really like movies." Dante pats my stomach gently. "Don't you worry your little head about it. We'll work it out."

I roll over to glare at him. "Worry my little head... who the fuck do you think you are–"

Dante interrupts me by slamming his mouth onto mine. An *oomf* escapes me, but then I quickly get with the program. God, the way Dante kisses is all-consuming. My entire body shuts down, all the oxygen trapped in my lungs. Delightful static fills my brain, like a television on a grayed-out channel. When Dante pulls away to bite at my throat, I bury my fingers in his hair and moan like the slut I am.

"I'll kill anyone that hurts you," Dante mumbles against my neck.

"What if *I* hurt me?" I ask softly, a shake to my voice.

Dante lifts up, elbows to either side of my head to stare down at me. "No more of that. Unless it's me hurting you." He trails a hand down my chest to swirl the pads of his fingers just under my belly button, fingers toying with the belly button ring he seems oddly obsessed with. I shiver helplessly and he grins, wide and cruel. "What if I hold a knife to your throat while we fuck? Would you like that?"

"You're insane," I whisper, heart beating wildly.

Dante dips down to whisper against my mouth, "And you like it."

Fuck me, I do. Dante kisses me until my brain is static again, then gives me the slowest, most indulgent blow job of my life. And when he jacks himself off and comes all over my face, I try to tell myself I don't like this at all. I don't get off on the idea of being owned by Dante. I don't feel a perverse and twisted joy when he says he'd murder for me.

———

THE AIR LOOKS CHILLY. Not that I'd know since I haven't been outside yet today. I'd like to go to school though, if only Dante could stop arguing about who is going to protect me when.

"I don't see why it can't be me," Dante grumbles, gaze stormy and aimed at Parker.

"Too invested. You'll make questionable decisions," Hayden explains with a dismissive wave of his hand. He smirks and looks at me over his shoulder. "Just let Parker do it. He's just as capable as you, Dante."

"Not with a gun," Dante says sourly.

"Excuse me?" Parker pipes up from where he leans against the kitchen counter, apple in the palm of his hand. "Let's go toe-to-toe at the range this weekend, buddy."

"Fuck you!"

"No, thank you," Parker says pleasantly.

Dante scowls and stomps over to stand in front of me. He takes my shoulders in the palms of his hands and shakes me a little. "Just when you leave the house, okay? If something happens to you, I'll cut off Parker's nuts, fry them, and make him eat them. So he will make sure no one touches you."

"No one but you," I say with a smirk.

Dante grins, pleased. "No one but me."

"No ball frying," Hayden orders just before disappearing back upstairs. There's a slam of a door, a shout, a tussle, then Parker sighs loudly and takes a large bite of his apple.

"Let's go. I have to write a paper while I sit outside your class," Parker says grumpily.

I watch as he trudges out the garage door, then Dante gently cups my face to turn my gaze back to his own. Dante's eyes are always so hard, but they're softer when he looks at me. I should hate it, should bite him for it, but a small part of me likes it. For Reid, the snarling twink.

"I'll be waiting here for you."

"I'm not going to war," I point out.

Dante hums, kisses my cheek, then shoves me toward the door that Parker just escaped through. The car is idling with the garage door open and Parker leans against the passenger side door, waiting for me to join him. Without a word, I climb in, pleased to know that it's cool enough outside to warrant the heater blasting. Parker fiddles with the stereo for a moment, before pulling out to make the annoying fifteen-minute drive to school. All of the lights, pedestrians, and hunting down a parking spot make driving an outright headache if you live as close to campus as we do. But I guess it's easier to protect me in the car than walking down the street.

"Can I smoke?" I ask while tugging the carton of cigarettes out of my pocket.

Parker grabs them, rolls the window down, and tosses them out with no fanfare. It all happens so fast that I can't even scream. I stare blankly out the window, then slowly shift my gaze to land on an unapologetic Parker.

"What the actual fuck?"

Parker rolls his eyes so hard I think they might get stuck. "They'll kill you."

"A meteor could hit right now and kill me."

"Yeah, well, that's out of your control," Parker says with all the patience of a parent explaining why their child can't have dessert. "No cigarettes while I'm on protection duty."

"I'm going to tell Dante."

Parker shrugs, uncaring. "Do it. I'm not scared of you or him."

Well, he should be scared of me. Anger threatens to boil over inside me the remainder of the drive to school, but I press it down as best I can. I'll just buy a new carton of smokes when I'm out of Parker's sight. I scramble out of the car the moment it's in park, ignoring Parker's hastily yelled *hey!* A few people turn to look at us as I hustle toward the math building with what I'm sure is a very annoyed-looking Parker racing to catch up with me.

I shove through the math building doors, not bothering to hold it open for him. A swear echoes through the front of the building and I grin in celebration as I climb the stairs two by two. The door to the classroom slams shut behind me. When I glance over my shoulder, Parker is absolutely seething, nostrils flared as he glares at me through the window. I send a wave over my shoulder, blow him a kiss, then pick my way through the desks to find my usual seat.

A few moments before class starts, my phone buzzes.

DANTE

don't be a little shit

this is who i am

DANTE

he's there to keep you safe

he threw away my cigarettes. tell him to replace them and I won't make his life miserable.

DANTE

fucking hell

see you later

DANTE

you don't have to make everything difficult

don't i? You like it

DANTE

fuck

🙂

WHEN I FINALLY EXIT THE math building in the afternoon, Parker leans casually against the brick wall with his laptop precariously balanced on one hand as he types furiously with the other. Instead of dodging him, I walk right up to him, and stop with my hand held out. Parker's jaw clenches, but he doesn't even attempt to argue. I can't help but grin when a familiar carton is pressed into my palm.

"Thank you ever so much," I say with a calculated grin.

Parker's eyes narrow. "You understand I'm keeping you alive, right?"

"Tomato, tomah-toe."

"I'm literally... you know what. I don't care. Go to the car so I can drive you back to the house. I'm switching with Jacob. I'll watch your brother while he watches over you. You want to be a little shit, the little shit can watch over you so that you guys can attempt to out–little shit each other."

"That's a lot of little shits," I reply with a mocking little frown. "Did I upset you?"

Parker's eyes twitch so badly that I'm momentarily afraid he's going to have a stroke or maybe a coronary. Instead, Parker takes a deep, slow breath, then turns around to head toward the parking lot. I follow behind him like a good boy because believe it or not, I don't have a death wish. The ride is once again totally silent. Parker doesn't even turn the radio on.

When he parks the car in the garage, he jumps out, comes around to my side and aggressively swings the door open. I gasp in shock when he bodily yanks me out of the SUV. I dig my feet into the ground but he's taller, and much broader, so I don't have much of a chance. The sound of voices from the kitchen reaches my ears before the sound of my blood boiling in my veins takes over.

Parker's grip on my arm is unforgiving. The voices cease talking when we step into the kitchen. Dante's eyes dart from me, to Parker's hand on my arm, to Parker's livid face. He moves quickly to cross the room, hand on my shoulder as he gets in Parker's face. I shiver at the intensity rolling off of him. I don't know if it's turning me on or frightening me, these days it seems to be a dangerous combination.

"Let him go," Dante orders, eyes hard on Parker.

"I cannot handle him. It'll have to be Jacob," Parker says, voice low but firm.

Jacob lifts his head from where he sits at the table. "But I've got the older brother."

"No. Switch with me."

Jacob and Parker stare each other down, before Jacob shrugs as if in awful acceptance of his punishment. I'm not *that* terrible.

"Dante..." I start, but slam my mouth shut when Dante stares me down.

"Alright, Parker," Dante says slowly, carefully minding his tone. "Jacob will watch Reid when he goes to campus. You can watch Mason."

Parker's jaw is still clenched tight when he nods tightly. Blood pounds in the spots where his fingers crushed my arm the moment he lets go. I rub awkwardly at my arm as Parker disappears up the stairs, the door to his room slamming loud enough to make me cringe.

"Why are you being so difficult?" Dante asks, teeth gritted in barely restrained fury. He's probably trying to scare me, but it actually oddly turns me on.

I open my mouth to reply, but nothing comes out. All words are frozen in my head, throat closed so not even a half-hearted attempt can escape.

"Oh, this just got too tense for me. I'm outtie," Jacob says before promptly exiting the room.

"Dante."

Dante shakes his head firmly. "No. Go upstairs."

My feet force me along before my brain can even process that I'm moving. The sound of Dante's feet climbing the stairs behind me should scare me, but they don't. Yeah, I'm being a brat. Normally I think it riles Dante up, but something about this situation is making it do the opposite. Maybe I grossly overplayed my hand. Maybe I fucked up, actually.

When we're safely ensconced in his room, I open my mouth to apologize, but Dante crowds me back against the door and presses his hand to my mouth. I'm trapped. My heart pounds wildly in my chest, like the wings of a hummingbird as they escape capture. Dante smells like he always does, like spice and a hint of sweat. His nostrils flare as he leers down at me, body poised to punish with how tight his muscles are coiled.

"Parker and Jacob's mother died of lung cancer," Dante says slowly, carefully enunciating each word so that it can get through my stupid, thick brain. "You cannot smoke around them or antagonize them about it. They were teens and she was a single mom. They lost fucking everything." My eyes widen as Dante presses his hand harder against my mouth. "You don't realize the shit you say... the shit you do... sometimes it's cute but sometimes it fucking hurts. You're so worried about punishing yourself for something you didn't even do that you end up punishing other people too. It's not okay. It's not, Reid. I... I have to make you learn."

Dante carefully pulls his hand away from my mouth while aiming a look at me that's so scathing, so disappointed, that my knees go a little weak. For the first time in my life the urge to speak isn't there at all. Anxiety boils at a low simmer inside me as I watch Dante pace the length of his room, his hands tangled tightly in his dark hair. He calms after a few moments, then turns his head to aim his sharp-eyed gaze on me.

His hands are firm on my shoulders as he gently pushes until I fall to my knees in the center of his room.

"Reid, you're a good boy, but you've done something very

bad, do you know that?" Dante asks while hurriedly fumbling around in his nightstand.

I duck my head in embarrassment and breathe slowly to keep the emotions at bay. I don't want to feel. Nothing at all. Just empty space inside my chest where a heart used to be. But goddamn if Dante hasn't been trying to make me feel the past few weeks. Feel things I told myself I never would.

Dante's bare feet reappear in my vision, but I don't lift my head. I can't meet his gaze, not now, not feeling like this, not feeling like I fucked everything up again. He dips down to be level with me, his hands carefully tracing down my arms, before gently tugging them behind me.

"Green, yellow, or red?" Dante asks softly, clearly seeking permission.

"Green, but... it could be yellow if... if you... you say mean things to me," I admit with a tremble in my voice.

"Okay," Dante replies gently, because somehow he knows me all the way to the deep dark pit of me. His hands roughly tug my wrists together, then hard cold metal snaps over my skin, and the sound of handcuffs makes my blood boil in fear, and a little excitement. "Still green?"

I nod, but Dante puts a finger under my chin to make me look at him. "Words."

"Green," I answer, tongue thick in my mouth.

"You're a good boy, but your behavior was very bad," Dante explains, voice carefully neutral, eyes sweet as always. "Do you know what you did that was wrong?"

I shake my head because I don't want to say the words out loud. Late afternoon sun slashes through the windows, casting light yellow and oranges through the room from behind the edges of Dante's blackout curtains.

Dante sighs softly, then tenderly strokes the skin under

my chin. His eyes smolder as he stares down at me. A split second passes by before he slowly dips down to press his lips against mine in a too-tender kiss. I lean forward, trying to get more of him, but he pulls away as if to tease me. I scowl, but Dante clicks his tongue.

"I'm doing this for you," Dante says with rare affection.

He stands abruptly, making me sway forward slightly at the loss of him. His bare foot presses against my knee hard until I'm sitting up straight, head tilted back to look up at him. My mouth goes dry at the glorious sight of him just before my heart pounds violently when he slowly backs away from me. His fingers clench and unclench painfully at his side a few times.

"Stay there until I tell you that you can get up."

And then he leaves the room. What the fuck? How would he even know if I stood up? He won't. I could get up right now, sit on the bed, walk around the room, and Dante would have no idea. But even though I could do that, I don't. I wiggle my fingers a few times, move my shoulders back as my arms go a little numb. My mouth is dry and I'm thirsty. I didn't even get to sneak a cigarette in after class because Parker was so mad.

No. He wasn't mad. He was furious. But I'd thought it'd been about *me*. It wasn't though, now that I can think about it clearly. I'd goaded him into purchasing cigarettes for me. The same thing that maybe killed his mom. I'm such a piece of shit. I know what it's like to lose a parent, I lost two. I can't even get on an airplane now because of that loss. Not sure if I'll ever be able to.

I miss my parents. I miss the way my mom gently woke me up before school with a kiss on my cheek and a whispered, "Time to get up, tootsie." I miss helping my dad in the backyard, just raking leaves, or planting the upcoming season's vegetables for my mother. When they died, it felt like the rug was pulled out from underneath me. I've been acting out for years. Fucking whoever is willing, drinking, taking random pills, even getting arrested once. The only person that ever even pretended to care was Mason and now Dante. Mason gave everything up to come back to Eastport, put me through school, and all I've done is terrify him.

My hands tingle with numbness now, sharp pinpricks that keep me from rolling away on the tide of sadness. I roll my shoulders again but it doesn't help. My hands and arms ache from the handcuffs, and my brain feels kind of scratchy, like a record with the needle in the wrong spot. The room slowly darkens as I sit there stewing in my own misery. This odd pain in my rib cage almost forces me over but I don't want to disappoint Dante. I can't disappoint another person.

The room darkens enough that the only light in the room is the glow of Dante's computer screen wallpaper. Blue carnations. Tiredness rolls over me in gigantic waves. I feel remade in a way. I'm like the shore as high tide comes in, all bad is going out, only for good to roll in.

Footsteps stop outside the bedroom, then seconds later the door pushes open and Dante's imposing figure cuts through the light from the hallway. He ignores me completely, moving around the room to prepare for bed. The odd urge to cry wells up inside me as he undresses down to just his boxers, disappears into the bathroom. Sounds of his nightly routine filter through the room, so comforting and familiar. Dante washes his face, brushes his teeth, swigs mouthwash, pees, then flips the bathroom light off to head toward the bed.

He's still ignoring me and for some reason that hurts more than anything.

Dante curls up in the middle of the bed, and I can just barely see the curve of his throat as he swallows.

That's when the tears start.

I try to hold them in but they won't stop. The dam has been broken. Fat, awful tears roll down my cheeks, landing on my parched lips. Sticking my tongue out, I lick them away, and that only makes me sob more because I want Dante to take care of me. No one ever takes care of me anymore.

I gasp as a sob tears through me. My vision blurs as I fight the urge to fall over. The room tilts dangerously on its axis. I'm melting into nothing, seeping into the earth, dark and damp inside me where something good should be. How can I be good? I want to be good... I want to be something worthy of love. I start to fall over but firm hands hold me tight. Dante is danger, but he's also safety.

The handcuffs fall away with a loud clunk. Dante's warm hands move up and down my arms, carefully tugging my wrists to sweetly hold them in his lap. I sway closer until my forehead is pressed against his broad chest. His hand comes up to gently hold my neck while I sob into his perpetually warm skin.

"I'm so sorry, Dante. I'm sorry. I didn't..." I gasp as the sobbing reaches a crescendo. I can't breathe. Every word is a hiccup. "I didn't mean, didn't want to... I don't want to hurt people. I hurt inside." I pull away and hit my chest as Dante stares down at me with real fear in his eyes. "Everything hurts all the time. I miss my mom and dad. I don't want to disappoint Mason anymore. I want to let you... let you take care of me. I want to stop being a fuckup. Help me stop being a fuckup. Please," I cry out, only for Dante to tug me back into his arms.

He stands in one quick movement and deftly carries me to the bed. When he tries to pull away, I reach out to grab on to him, hysterical and unwilling to let him go. All of the emotions are too much, I don't know what to do with them. Where do all the emotions go when I can't burn them away? Dante shushes me, but climbs into the bed. I cry for I don't know how long, until my head is pounding and I feel like all the bad thoughts bled out of me to leave me renewed. Dante's hand glides gently up and down my back in a soothing motion that renders me even more lightheaded than the crying did.

"Reid... tell me your color."

"Green," I whisper.

"You did so good... you waited for me like a good boy." Dante dips down so that our gazes lock and he smiles, that real smile that feels like it's only mine. He gently wipes tears from my cheek with the edge of the pillowcase. "You're so perfect when you let yourself be. So good. I'm so proud of you for doing what I said. Okay?"

I nod quickly, feeling like I might cry again. Dante leans down to kiss me sweetly, almost a promise, but not a vow. When he pulls away, he spends the next few moments carefully undressing me. I close my eyes under his tender ministrations. He rolls away for a second to return with a bottle of sports drink in his hand and a chocolate bar. Once he's manhandled me between his spread legs, he feeds me bits of chocolate and sips of the grape-flavored drink. I hum softly between each bite and swallow until the chocolate is gone and the drink is half empty.

Dante keeps me between his legs, back pressed against

his chest. His hands skim over my chest, to my scarred stomach, my arms, then my thighs. I feel floaty and tired, like the world would disappear if I blinked too hard. I wouldn't mind as long as I was in the safe net of Dante's arms.

"It's going to be okay," Dante promises.

For the first time in a long time, I agree.

———

EVERYTHING HURTS when I blink my eyes open the next morning. Inside I feel like a marshmallow that spent too long on the fire and outside I feel like I ran three marathons back-to-back.

"Ugh," I groan while stretching out my limbs.

"Careful," Dante murmurs while gently resting his hand over my stomach. "Do you want some coffee? Breakfast?"

I hum and roll over to shelter myself in his arms. A grin inches its way over my lips when his arms immediately circle around me. This is safety.

"Scrambled eggs with sourdough toast, apricot jam, and lots of cheese in the eggs, please. And coffee."

Dante chuckles. He presses a kiss against my forehead before silently leaving the bedroom to scrounge up something as close to my request as he can find. I fall back asleep while waiting, only rousing when Dante's weight tugs his side of the bed down. Squinting up at him, he smiles and wiggles a mug of coffee in front of my face. That does the trick.

I sit up and gratefully take the coffee. The sweet nectar of the gods almost burns my tongue, but I don't care at this point. Dante removes the mug from my hands after a few decadent sips, only to slowly start feeding me the eggs. Jacob must've made them because they're fluffy, with just the right amount of cheese. The toast is already perfectly smeared with butter and apricot jam as if Dante had it all lying in wait before I even said a word.

"You're good at this," I mumble around a mouthful of food.

Dante raises one eyebrow. "At what?"

"Taking care of me after..." I do an odd hand motion that I hope he'll understand. Dante's eyes sparkle and his lips curve up in a half-smile. "You know."

"I've never been like this with someone before... you bring it out in me. We're both learning new things."

"Don't learn too much and then think the grass is greener somewhere else."

Dante frowns. "You're the only grass I want."

"Oh?" I ask as he feeds me another bite of eggs.

He blushes slightly and avoids my eyes. "Don't make me say it."

"Okay."

We finish breakfast, then take a long, very sweet shower. Dante pointedly ignores my hard cock and his own, and I wonder if that's a sort of lingering punishment that I should start to expect after he's taught me a lesson. Dressed in a pair of my own sweats and one of Dante's faded band tees, I descend the stairs to face the choir.

All the boys are in the kitchen. Jacob's washing dishes at the sink, while Parker reads at the table with a piece of toast between his fingers, and Hayden is typing away at his laptop with a very angry sort of look on his beautiful face.

Dante clears his throat so that they all look up, then glances at me. Oh. Right.

"I am... sorry... about yesterday," I say through gritted teeth.

Parker lifts one bushy eyebrow. "Sorry for what?"

Oh, Jesus Christ.

"Being a little shit. I won't smoke anymore."

Parker hums, then returns to his book as if totally disinterested with my apology. Dante should teach *him* a lesson. Wait, no. I don't like that. Dante is only allowed to teach me lessons. But someone else should definitely teach Parker a lesson because he's obnoxious.

Jacob finishes at the sink, then salutes us all. He disappears upstairs, leaving a frowning Hayden staring after him.

"Mason appears to be leaving the house today, so I'll be tracking him." Parker aims a steely look at me. "I placed a very heavy security system around your house on top of your subpar one that looks fancy but doesn't actually do shit. It was hard bugging the place while Mason was there. You both don't have as many survival instincts as you should, you know. He slept through me breaking into the house."

"You broke into my *house*," I squawk.

Parker disappears through the front door without a worry about my fury. I turn to Dante with narrowed eyes, but Dante just shrugs.

"You said to keep Mason safe," Dante points out as if my fury doesn't matter to him one bit. "You're here. Gotta do it some way. Now, I have class today, so be a good boy and work on your homework here. Okay?"

I flush at being called a good boy in front of Hayden, but nod anyway. I will be a good boy. Because maybe that means Dante will come home and treat me well. Maybe. When Dante disappears out the front door with his backpack slung over his shoulder, I'm left alone with a still furiously typing Hayden. Scully sits in his lap, purring, and every now and then Hayden pauses to rest his hand on her head and give her a little scratch. It's cute. Maybe they're both psychos and she's his familiar.

"What are you working on?" I ask because I'm nosier than my self-preservation instincts allow.

"I'm trying to steal half a million dollars from this pharmaceutical company that stole a patent from someone for a treatment for multiple sclerosis," Hayden explains while still typing. He chews his bottom lip and squeezes one eye shut. "Obviously you're sworn to secrecy or I'll kill you."

"About what you're doing now or... all of it."

Hayden pauses to glare at me. "All of it."

I shrug. "Who am I going to tell? I don't have any friends and my brother wouldn't believe me. Also, I'm on your side. Capitalism is evil."

"Is that why you're okay with all of this?"

Is it? I don't know. I think about it for a moment while Hayden returns to typing.

"Maybe, but also maybe there's a little part of me that just likes the chaos."

Hayden snorts. "You are a chaos gremlin, for sure. Do you know anything about Linux?"

"What language?"

Hayden lifts his head slowly to look at me for what feels like very fresh eyes. He leans forward slightly in his chair with an assessing sort of look.

"Ruby."

I wiggle my fingers at his computer. "Give me."

Hayden frowns, looks down at his computer, then pushes it toward me with one finger. I squint at the screen, desperately trying to understand what he's doing. It's the backend of a program for sure, but it looks like he's trying to kill it without someone being able to find the death switch.

"Are you trying to make this defunct?"

"Yes."

"I thought you were stealing money from a pharmaceutical company."

Hayden huffs in frustration. "I can't just hack into their bank account and steal it back. Instead, I'm crashing an app the CEO invested money into so that when the stock market opens tomorrow, it'll open low enough to scare investors into selling in mass."

"Devious," I compliment with an impressed smile.

Hayden sits up straighter. "Thank you."

Hayden and I spend the afternoon passing the laptop back and forth until we've dismantled the app from being able to work properly, even with the fail-safes in place. By the time we're satisfied with the destruction, Jacob is wandering in to start cooking dinner. He takes one look at the two of us cozied up at the table together and sighs dramatically.

"Can I help?" I blurt out while Jacob's head is buried in the fridge.

Jacob aims an odd look at me over his shoulder. "I guess. Can you chop vegetables?"

"I'm pretty good with knives," I say with a leer.

Jacob stares blankly back at me. "Okay."

I join Jacob at the counter. He slides a cutting board in front of me, then plops down potatoes in a variety of colors. He tells me to chop them into quarters, so that's what I do. It's mindless, makes my brain shut off much like working on the coding with Hayden did. I have sets of equations to do as homework, but I think this matters more.

9

DANTE

The house smells so heavenly that my mouth waters the moment I walk inside. As I take off my shoes by the front door, I realize it's the scent of herbs, onions, and butter wafting from the kitchen. My gut tightens when I walk in to find Reid helping Jacob cook dinner. Hayden is sitting at the table with his fingers tangled on top, head tilted as he also watches the two men interact.

Something about Reid here with us feels so right that it's a little frightening. Like maybe we've been waiting for him to come along to even out our odds. Hayden's gaze is fixed on Jacob's back, tracking his movement as the other man moves around the kitchen with obvious intent. A timer goes off and I watch with my heart in my throat as Reid slips on an oven mitt, opens the oven, then tugs out roasted potatoes. The domesticity of the moment overwhelms me.

Jacob flips over steaks that are sizzling in a cast-iron pan on the stove. He murmurs something to Reid, points at the steak, then jiggles one a little with his fork. Reid smiles and nods while giving Jacob his undivided attention.

Quietly as I can, I pull out the chair beside Hayden and join him in staring. Jacob's carefully honed senses clock the sound though, because he glances over his shoulder toward us. He grins at me, then flushes under Hayden's scrutiny and turns back to Reid. They gather plates, then place meat and potatoes on them.

"Parker said he'll be late," Jacob apologizes on his twin's behalf. "He'll eat leftovers from the other night."

Reid's eyebrows quirk in confusion, but he stays quiet instead of interrogating Jacob. I wrap my arm around the back of Reid's chair after he takes a seat. We're all quiet as he digs into the perfectly seasoned dinner. Reid lets out these little hums as he eats that make the base of my spine tingle with need. He only eats about a quarter of his steak before pushing his plate away.

I go to tell him to eat more, but one look from Reid shuts me up. Oh. Suddenly, I don't want to eat my entire meal either. Our eyes stay locked for a moment, before I stand abruptly, my chair scraping awkwardly against the floor. Jacob and Hayden stare at me in confusion, then quickly lose interest when I awkwardly clear my throat, grab Reid by the arm, and drag him bodily up the stairs.

"What—"

I don't let Reid finish. I shove him down onto the bed and devour his mouth with single-minded focus. He laughs against my mouth while curling his arms around the back of my neck. His skin is hot beneath my touch, warming me from the outside after the past few days. I have this insane urge to mark him, make sure it's clear to everyone that he's mine. The fuckers trying to take him from me will die by a thousand cuts before they even have a chance to touch him. I swear that on all my belongings. On my life.

Reid's cock is hard as he rocks up into me, moaning softly against my mouth.

"You were so good last night, so good today. Such a good boy."

Reid mewls underneath me, his fingers sneaking under my shirt to rake painfully down my back. I latch on to his neck and bite hard, almost hard enough to draw blood, and the sharp bite of my teeth makes Reid go wild beneath me. He bucks his hips up so our cocks roughly slide together through our clothes. All control bleeds out of me.

"Please, please, please," Reid all but sings.

God. I lift onto my knees to hastily drag my shirt over my head. The way Reid stares up at me makes all the blood in my body boil at once. I need to be inside him now. Make him see how much he means to me. How much I always fucking want him even though none of this makes a lick of sense.

We make quick work of getting me out of the rest of my clothes, then get him undressed. Reid laughs when I blow a raspberry on his scarred belly, but it turns into a low moan when I lick just below his belly button. I spend a few minutes giving attention to his belly button ring, urging deep, guttural moans out of Reid. I stare up at him as I slowly take his cock into my mouth, feeling like a king when his mouth opens on a silent scream. His hands fumble on the sheets for a moment as if unsure what to do, where he can put them. I can't have that. Grabbing his hands, I gently place them on top of my head, and that shatters a loud, borderline-violent moan out of Reid.

He fucks up into my mouth without any finesse. The taste of him explodes on my tongue, warmth and musk and *Reid*. I lick the head of his cock, smiling around it when his thighs quake with pleasure. He throws an arm over his eyes as if to ensure he can't watch me take him apart, like the pleasure's too much to handle. Reaching a hand up, I fumble under the pillow until it latches on to the lube.

Reid moans low and long when I slowly press a lubed finger into him. I work his cock over languidly in my mouth, just enough to take the focus off of getting some lube into him. God, he's so fucking tight. I need to be inside him already. His head is tossed back, tendons tight enough to snap as his mouth hangs open from the pleasure of the moment.

I crawl up his body, two fingers still inside him, and take his mouth in a bruising kiss. His tongue duels with mine for a moment, giving the illusion of a fight, before he falls back to letting me own his mouth as per usual. I nip at his lips as I hitch his hips up my waist and notch my cock against his greedy hole. He's so fucking tight when I press in that his breath stutters in his lungs.

"Dante," Reid whispers, head still tossed back in pleasure. His fingers rake down my back, searching for purchase as I bottom out inside him. "Dante, Dante, fuck me."

"Fuck, look at the way you take me."

That gorgeous red flush works its way down Reid's chest as he pants up at me. Starry-eyed and needy, this is my very favorite kind of Reid. I sit for as long as I can, the control slowly bleeding out of me. When Reid borderline cries, trying to urge me on with his heels, I let go.

I can't deny Reid a single ounce of pleasure, not with that maroon flush stealing down his pale chest, not when his lip is caught between his teeth, not when he wants but doesn't know how to ask for his desires. I snap my hips forward so hard that his head thumps against the headboard. Reid's eyes roll back in his skull and he's lost to the pleasure. We're just slapping skin, bitten-down moans, and desperate kisses as I fuck him into the cloud-soft mattress. His legs tighten around my hips after each thrust as if to keep me inside him, as if he can't stand the momentary loss of me.

Sweat prickles my skin as I fuck into him as hard as I can, surely hard enough to make him feel it for days. A fierce pleasure settles in me at the idea of Reid feeling me days from now, knowing that he's mine to give pleasure to, to take pleasure from. Reid's all fucking mine.

"I'm gonna put a baby in you," I pant above him, not knowing where the words even came from. "Breed you so everyone knows you're mine."

Definitely a shot in the dark, but the words make Reid go supernova. His back bends off the bed as he comes untouched, his mouth slack, eyes shut tight as his body succumbs to orgasm. It's the hottest thing I've ever seen. I pummel into him, fucking him through his orgasm and seeking my own. Grabbing his thigh, I hitch it up higher and press my forehead to his as the telltale tingle at the base of my spine starts to signal my orgasm. My cock spasms inside Reid moments before a violent orgasm crashes through me. Pouring every ounce of myself inside him, hips twitching even as I stop thrusting and fall on top of him.

Reid's arms wrap around me, his fingers lovingly carding through my sweaty hair. We lie like that for a while, just enjoying each other's bodies, our breaths easing after the ferocity of our orgasms.

I bury my face in Reid's sweaty neck. Swiping my hands up and down his sides, I stay inside him until I slip out. Reid whines at the loss, so I sneak my hand down to roughly shove two fingers inside him, keeping my cum where he wants it.

"You always know what I need," Reid murmurs, words post-orgasm slurred.

"Yeah, I do."

I lay my head against his chest, listening to his pounding heartbeat slowly return to normal. He moves his leg slightly to rub at my side in a movement that has my chest constricting with want, despite already having fucked him senseless. After a while I get us both up and into the shower to rinse off. I like Reid in moments like this, when he's less feisty spitfire, and more sweet boy. He leans against my chest, head tilted back against my shoulder as the water trails a river down our bodies, cleansing us of our sins. He lets me gently wash his hair, eyes closed, a sweet smile on his lips. Reid returns the favor back to me, on his tiptoes so that he can reach. Somehow that makes him even more endearing to me.

We dry each other off, then brush our teeth to get ready for bed.

"The picture of the woman on your desk?" Reid asks, eyes curious, mouth full of toothpaste.

Oh. "Ama, my older sister."

Reid lifts an eyebrow. "And?"

I dip my head and spit out my toothpaste, keeping my head bowed to avoid looking at him in the mirror. Gripping the edge of the counter, I close my eyes tight against the thoughts of her.

"She was in a car accident when she was sixteen... she was on her way to pick me up from track practice. A truck driver didn't see her car... it was a mistake. Wasn't his fault. But she sustained a traumatic brain injury, so now she's permanently disabled." I close my eyes tighter to prevent the tears from falling. "The insurance company denied a lot of things for her... my mom was a stay-at-home mom, so it was just my dad's insurance from when he worked at a mechanic shop and it wasn't very good. Now she's on disability, which also isn't very good. My parents make do with what they can... but Ama's life will never be the same. It is hard to lose someone, but they are still here. It's a different type of grief. Now... now a lot of my payment for all this goes toward making sure she's in a state-of-the-art care facility back home. My parents don't have to work as hard, and Ama is safer, happier where she is. That's all that matters, that Ama is safe."

Reid's hand rubs up and down my back in a comforting glide. He moves his body closer to me, side pressed against my arm, because he knows I need the comfort of the warmth of his skin. I take a few deep breaths, then stand up to look down at him. His mouth is bunched to the side, searching eyes flicking between mine.

"Is that why you do this?"

I shrug, because I don't know. "Do I need a reason beyond wanting bad people to pay for bad deeds?"

"No, I guess not," Reid answers truthfully. He dances his fingers up my back to lovingly tangle in the hair at the base of my neck. "I like you so much. Don't hurt me."

"I won't hurt you. I promise."

Reid smiles shakily, then leans up on his toes to kiss me. We kiss like that for a while, soft and slow, sweet kisses that make my toes curl against the cold tile. Finally, we pull apart and I switch the bathroom light off, then follow Reid into the bed. We lie side by side for a while, staring up at the dark ceiling, no words exchanged between us. Two broken boys, hurt by the world, finding an odd comfort with each other. If soulmates exist, I think Reid would be mine.

Hayden bursts into the room panting, bringing bright light from the hallway with him.

"Parker's tracker went off, I got an alert."

I sit up straight in the bed, heart pounding. "What do you mean?"

Hayden frantically waves his phone at me. "Gone, a few minutes ago."

A loud crash from Jacob's bedroom sounds, then he's stumbling towards us. "I feel sick." And then he promptly pukes all over the hallway floor. What the fuck.

Hayden glances at him in concern, hand twitching to reach out, before yanking away to turn his gaze back to me. "We've got to move."

I glance over at Reid, leaning forward to kiss him hard, I pull away with my hand wrapped around his chin. "You have to stay here."

"I'll come with you," Reid says defiantly, eyes blazing.

"Absolutely not. Stay here."

I climb out of the bed before my brain can make a bad decision like allowing Reid to come with us, where I can't effectively protect him. I hurry to get dressed in an ops outfit, harness over my shirt with two guns strapped in, knives in my cargo pants pockets. When I'm finally done and exiting the closet, I find Reid grumpily cleaning up Jacob's puke.

He shakes his head when I look at him in wonder. Jacob and Hayden are gone, probably getting ready for the scrambled mission.

"I–"

"Shut up," Reid says, nostrils flaring. "I'll see you when you get back. Okay?"

"Yeah. Listen, we have a panic room. I have to put you in there."

"What?" Reid screeches. "No... you can't. I'm claustrophobic."

Well, that isn't going to make this easy, then. I roughly grab Reid by the bicep and drag him toward the other end of the floor, kicking and screaming. I slap my hand against the wall to open it up and shove Reid inside when the hidden door slides open. Reid stares at me from the ground, wide-eyed and frightened, but I'll do whatever I have to do to keep him safe. Including breaking his trust. Scully rushes into the room beside Reid, and Reid's hand instinctively goes out to touch her. Usually she hisses or spits at me, but not this time. Oddly, her animal eyes say she's got this, got him, and I pray that I'm doing the right thing.

I leave him kneeling in the safe room because if I don't, I'll say something stupid, like tell him how much I love him and want to marry him. Silence envelops me when the door to the safe room slams shut, and I force myself to back away, to leave him there. Jacob and Hayden are already standing downstairs in their own tactical gear. Hayden's hand is wrapped around Jacob's neck, squeezing gently while Jacob sways back and forth.

"Ready to go?"

Hayden removes his hand so fast it looks like he's been burned. Jacob looks green around the gills, tanned skin a few shades lighter than normal, eyes a little glassy. I'm not sure he's fit for a mission but there's no way I can keep him from checking on Parker. Jacob and I head toward our bikes, and Hayden hops onto Jacob's bike behind him, arms tight around Jacob's waist.

The night is cold, clouds passing over the full moon as we make the quick ride to Mason's house. Parking a block away, we walk the rest of the way quickly under the shadow of darkness. I'm already concerned when Parker isn't posted up outside in a usual spot we'd pick while watching someone. The front door pushes open without any fight, making Jacob gasp in fear behind me.

"I'd stay out here with Jacob… in case," I order Hayden, not even finishing my sentence because he knows.

Hayden goes pale, but lifts his arm to grip Jacob's shoulder firmly. Jacob's pulse visibly pounds in his neck. That's the last thing I see before easing into the house. The kitchen light is on, but the rest of the house is quiet. Slipping one of my guns out of the harness, I creep toward the kitchen after I've cleared the downstairs living room.

I freeze in the hallway as I take in the sight of Parker passed out cold on the ground, and Mason tied up in a chair. Duct tape is over his mouth and tears slide down his cheeks. I rip the duct tape off and Mason heaves in gulps of air.

"They touched me, they touched me," Mason repeats over and over while shaking his head. "Dante, grab that pill bottle. Now. Please, fuck."

My frantic gaze lands on a prescription bottle on the counter. I grab the bottle, about to open the lid but Mason mewls loudly. Looking back at him, his eyes are glassy, lips trembling at the sight of me with the bottle. I don't know what to fucking do. Instinct takes over. I cut him loose from the zip ties around his ankles and wrists behind the chair.

Mason lurches forward to grab the bottle. Opening it, he tips it back so two pills fall into his mouth and he swallows them dry. Slumping in the chair, his stomach shakes as he fights to inhale, his fingers twitching in his lap. Fuck.

"What the fuck happened?" I ask. I dip down to check the bump on the side of Parker's head. Fuck, they hit him hard. After a cursory check of his body, I'm pleased that all else seems to be fine. I roll him over gently onto his back, dropping my head down to listen to his breathing. He's fine. He'll wake up with a headache but that's the best scenario here.

Mason has calmed already, but his hands still tremble in his lap. "I need to wash my hands." He stands on shaky legs and goes to the sink, diligently washing his hands four times. His shoulders lower from around his ears, then he spins around to stare at me. "I was cooking dinner, getting ready to do some work this afternoon. Two men in masks barged into the door dragging this guy with them. They tied me up, asked me questions but I..." Mason pauses and takes a deep breath. "I have terrible OCD, and when they touched me, it triggered me, so I was effectively useless. Didn't give them anything they wanted. But they mentioned Reid's name before they left... what have you got my brother tangled up in?"

All of my blood runs cold.

"They mentioned Reid?" I ask quietly, voice shaking.

Mason squints at me. "Yes. Where is he? Isn't he with you?"

Oh, fuck. I run out of the house like a bat fleeing hell. Jacob and Hayden scream after me, but I can't think of anything beyond getting back to Reid. I don't even remember the ride back to the house. It's been maybe thirty minutes since I left Reid behind. The bike skids to a halt in front of the house and I don't even bother with the kickstand. Just climb off the bike and let it fall to the ground to take the stairs two at a time.

"Reid!" I scream.

If something happens to Reid because of me, I'll kill myself. I'll never let myself feel an ounce of joy ever again.

The empty house echoes back to me. My heart pounds violently as I climb the stairs two by two. I pause for a moment, afraid to find what my instincts shout at me. I should've let him come with us, should've kept him safe beside me. Gritting my teeth, I slap my hand against the wall, and gasp when the hidden door whips open. No Reid. Holy fuck. Scully races out of the room, hair sticking up, tail straight to the sky. I end up back in the kitchen, spinning around with my head in my hands. That's how Hayden finds me when he bursts through the front door. A few moments later Jacob, Mason, and Parker come in behind him. Parker is still kind of out of it, an ice pack pressed to his head.

"Reid?" Hayden asks wearily. He dips down to pick up Scully, gripping her tight as she mewls and digs her claws into him for protection. Fuck.

"I... he's not here." I fight against the urge to sob. "He's not here. I don't get it... they didn't take Mason or Parker... what did they want?"

Parker winces at my voice. "They wanted Reid. We were a distraction."

My stomach drops at his point, because it sounds right.

Hayden steps past me, eyes caught on the dining table. His fingers reach out, but hastily pull away. My eyes follow his hand to see the piece of paper on the table. The paper is perfectly white, ink black and typed out, looking as if it was pulled directly from the printer before being plopped on the table.

"YOU ALL WILL PAY *for your crimes. You take from others, so now I will take from you.*"

. . .

"IT'S NOT EVEN A RANSOM LETTER..." Hayden trails off to lift his scared blue gaze to mine. "What the fuck do they want?"

"You've got to tell Robin... we've done so much. It's our turn to be helped. If something happens to Reid..." I blow out a breath, squeezing my eyes shut. "I'll burn this city to the ground if one single hair on his head is hurt."

Mason gasps loudly. "You care about him that much?"

I swallow roughly. "I'd fucking kill for him. He's mine. Take that how you will."

Parker moans loudly from the living room. "They smelled like the guys from the one job. The one where we killed the guy and returned all the money in his bank account to the people he'd stolen it from. The club owner."

"What?" Hayden asks around a laugh. "You remember them from the way they smell?"

Parker shrugs lightly before moaning. "Clove cigarettes and salami."

Hayden squeezes his eyes shut tightly, then pulls out his phone to type away. He collapses at the table and Jacob joins him, their bodies pressed tightly together as Jacob keeps a wary eye on his twin. Mason stands uncomfortably by the front door, eyes darting around the room. I haven't cleaned in a while, so it's messier than normal, but we're not dirty guys. It's a normal lived-in house, but Mason's cheeks take on a flush as he wraps his arms tightly around himself.

"Please find my brother soon," Mason pleads.

"I'll tear the world apart to find him," I promise, meaning every word.

Hayden quickly stands from the table, chair screeching against the tile floor. He heads outside into the night, voice hush-quiet as he whispers on the phone. I feel anxious and out of it while I wait for some sort of hint, some way to find Reid.

What if I can't find him? What if someone *hurts* him? What if he's crying out for me, waiting for me to save him, as the minutes tick by without me bursting through the door. So many what-ifs run through my brain that I start to feel sick with it. I dip down in a squat, cradling my head in my hands as I almost vomit from the emotions sweeping through me. I've got to get to Reid before someone tries to hurt him. I've got to tell him that I love him.

10

REID

That motherfucker locked me in the safe room or panic room whatever he wants to fucking call it. I squeeze my eyes shut tight as the nauseating dizziness overtakes me, the thrum of the anxiety of being shut in a room without any escape. Scully tries to calm me, pressing her slight black body against my face when I fall to the floor in a ball. My heart is pounding so hard in my chest that I assume it's going to stop beating altogether. This is it. I die in a safe room instead of by taking random pills, by seeking out dangerous men in clubs that only see me as a fleeting good time. This is how I die and how it all ends.

Tears fall from my eyes as I weep all my fears away. Dante will come back for me. He won't leave me locked in here forever. Dante loves me, I know it. The way he looks at me has to be love. Dante... come back.

"Please," I whimper into Scully's soft fur.

She purrs loudly as she rubs all over my face and oddly it distracts me enough for my heart to start to slow, for the tears to turn to a gentle stream instead of a torrential river. How long will it take him to come back for me? Why is someone trying to get to him through me? Jesus, if someone hurt Mason and I survive... what a cruel twist of fate. He survives childhood cancer just to die because I got twisted up in something that I'm not able to handle.

I roll over onto my back gasping, blinking up at the bright white lights that flicker in the room that's no longer closing in on me. Scully moves from my face to lie on my chest, kneading biscuits on my chest with her little bean paws. God. I curl my fingers into her soft fur, probably harder than she'll like, no doubt she'll hiss and claw soon. But she doesn't. No. Scully just purrs louder to distract me, nuzzling her soft head against my chin until I can't be anything but solely focused on her. Smart girl.

"Almost like you have experience with this stuff, girl." I pet her slowly, letting the feel of her hair against my sweaty palm distract me from my current predicament. Gradually, as I pet her, my heart slows enough that the anxiety of being stuck disappears just enough to make me feel less insane than a few moments ago. Maybe being trapped here won't kill me. I still hate it, I'm still going to murder Dante for this, but maybe I can live through this.

A sound from outside the door has me scrambling up, clutching Scully in my arms. She meows loudly at the sudden movement, and I scramble into the corner to protect my back. My anxiety ramps up again when I hear furious shouting and what sounds like banging coming from outside. Oh. That's not Dante. That's not the boys. They would've opened the door and let me out already. Scully seems to know it too because her claws press into me, making me hiss at the sensation.

The lights flicker just as the door slips open to reveal two very large men with black masks over their faces. They smell disgusting. I am totally fucked. One inches forward, eyes lit up with the glory of a win. Do I fight or do I give in? What's the easiest way to avoid murder? Instincts say for me to bite their balls off, but that's probably not the best way to go about this.

The man lunges for me before I can even come up with another escape idea. Scully yowls loudly, hisses, and bites the guy, but he just grabs her by the scuff and slings her against the wall of the panic room.

"No!" I scream, terrified that he just hurt Scully. I can't see her over his back, but I glare at him in fury that I can't hold back any longer. "You're fucking with the wrong people."

"Give me a break," the guy sneers, just before jabbing a needle into my neck.

Oh no.

I try to lunge at him, but my arms are too weak, and the walls are seriously closing in now. The last thing I hear is the men's soft laughter as I fall into a hazy, scary sort of sleep. Dante...

———

Drip. Drip. Drip.

The world is a blurry mess when I blink my eyes open. Everything hurts. Not in the fun way I've gotten used to either. I kind of feel like how I used to feel after taking those random pills at clubs. Wrung out and achy. The urge to puke is so overwhelming suddenly that I roll over onto my side and hurl straight up stomach acid. Yuck.

Wait. Why am I on the ground? Why is it concrete? I squeeze my eyes shut tightly, then carefully sit up despite the ache of my muscles. My arm catches on something, and when I look down, it's to find I'm chained to a metal pillar in the middle of some large room. Squinting against the bright light, I follow the length of the pillar to the ceiling above that's got holes in it from age. So much rust. When's the last time I had my tetanus shot? Mason is going to be furious if I die from tetanus, an easily preventative disease.

I take in my surroundings, wondering where the fuck I am and how I got here. It appears I'm in a beaten-down and ancient warehouse. Mostly empty, since it's just me, the holes in the ceiling, and the handcuffs chaining me to the metal pillar. Now the small pile of stomach acid to my right. Where the hell am I? I don't remember anything from the night before. Well. I remember Dante fucking me into oblivion, then everything gets kind of blurry after that. But that's kind of normal considering the shit we get up to.

The warehouse door opens with a rusty metallic sound that makes me cringe, to reveal a large guy wearing a ski mask. Oh. That does not inspire good feelings. He stops a few feet away from me, nose scrunched in obvious distaste at the smell of the vomit beside me.

"Oops?"

The guy scowls. "I'm not cleaning that up."

"No problem, just unlock the handcuffs and I'll do it."

"Fat chance," the guy drawls, foot tapping as he stares impatiently down at me. "You're collateral."

He tosses a bottle of water and a granola bar at my feet, just barely missing the puddle of puke. I reach out for it with my free hand, then glance up at him.

"I'm not good collateral. No one's going to miss me."

"Not even Dante?"

My blood goes cold. So that's the game we're playing now.

"I don't know who you're talking about. But I'll tell you that torture won't work on me because I like that shit."

"Weirdo," the guy mumbles before marching out the warehouse doors.

Jeez. I tentatively sip at the water, then make myself eat a few bites of the granola. Even though they said I'm not going to be hurt, I don't know when they'll change their mind. This could be the last meal I get for a long time for all I know. I wonder if they have cameras in here watching me?

I shift around on the cold concrete, letting the handcuffed arm hang loosely at my side while picking at the granola bar. When I shift, I feel the telltale lump of my cell phone in my back pocket. Are these guys total fucking idiots? My phone is still on me. I wonder how long it'll take Dante to realize that I put software on his phone so that I can track him. And that I also put it on my phone so that he can track me. See, this is what I get for being sneaky. If I had just *told* him I was being a possessive weirdo, he'd probably already be on his way here to save me.

The warehouse door slams open again to reveal a different guy than last time. This guy is huge, built like a brick house, and he's carrying a steel briefcase. That's odd. Suddenly, I kind of regret eating and drinking because I have the urge to hurl again.

The man kneels slowly at my feet, movements precise and military-like with their efficiency. He unlocks the suitcase to reveal surgical instruments. Oh no. I am way out of my league here. No amount of shit talking or sarcasm is going to make this end remotely well for me. Suddenly I really miss Dante and Mason. Although the idea of Mason being trapped in a place like this makes me feel even sicker, because it would probably send him into cardiac arrest.

"Do you want to know what their nickname for me is?" the guy asks with a thick Russian accent.

"Hot stuff?" I say with a crack in my voice.

The guy lifts his head to grin at me. "My second nick-name, I guess. I am The Carver, but you can call me Claude. Very nice to meet you, Reid. This will be easy if you do not struggle. Do you understand?"

"Do I look like someone that's not going to struggle?"

Claude tilts his head like a predator eyeing their prey. "No, perhaps you don't. But I will enjoy it more if you struggle, okay?"

"I don't know *anything*. There is no point in torturing me."

Claude hums before tugging a very sharp-looking scalpel out of the traveling torture suitcase. He leans forward a little, gaze sweeping over me in a way that makes my skin prickle with unease.

"Stand," Claude orders.

I do not stand. His eyes squint dangerously before he grabs my arm and yanks me up. Holding the scalpel against my throat, he presses his hands over me, grunting in victory when he finds my phone. He slams it to the ground, then crunches it under his steel-toed boot. I mewl softly, suddenly realizing I have lost my last fucking hope of being found.

Claude lifts his head and grins through his mask. "I am dealing with fucking amateurs here, but I am not paid big money to allow little mistakes. Now for each lie you tell me, I will cut either a very important appendage off or slice into that very pretty skin. Do you understand?"

My body shakes, but I maintain my glare at him because even under pressure, I am always going to be a little shit. Dante would be proud of me. If he ever knows. God, I hope he's keeping Mason safe. Sourness rises up in my throat at the thought of Mason, the thought of leaving him with absolutely no one in this world. I'm going to kill myself through the power of my mind alone.

"No puking," Claude says firmly, like he's ordering my body to listen. "It grosses me out."

"But blood is okay?" I ask weakly.

"Blood is normal human function. Puking is unpredictable with lots of chunks sometimes since they gave you food. Do not do it. Be good boy and hold it in. This will be quick if you just tell me what I need to know." Claude points at the ground, making his tight long-sleeve shirt ride up to reveal an intricate-looking tattoo. "Lie down."

I lower myself to the ground with shaky legs. He carefully arranges my limbs so that I resemble a starfish, head tilting this way and that until he's got me exactly how he wants me. Claude spends a few moments snapping on latex gloves, then carefully slides my shirt up my abdomen. He takes a few moments to stare at the ladder of scars on my stomach, then at the carefully placed lines on my thighs.

He hums, then lifts the scalpel. "This will not feel good because you are not controlling it. My apologies." He chuckles, ruefully shaking his head at his own joke. God. What a weirdo. "Such a weird saying. I am not really sorry, but it felt nice to say. Do you know who Dante and the others work for?"

"No," I say softly, voice trembling. My stomach quivers as he lowers the scalpel to press against my skin. "No, I really don't. I swear. I don't know anything. I just know... I just know that someone sends them tasks to do."

Claude pauses with the scalpel against my skin. His thumb presses down on my stomach, while his index finger presses down on the scalpel. When I breathe in, the scalpel barely slices my skin, but he doesn't use pressure to push down. I watch distantly as small dots of blood pool on my abdomen. Oh. He's right.

"I really don't know," I say with a tremble in my voice. I'm so scared, not in the way that's safe with Dante. But in the sort of way where death feels really imminent and I don't know what to do. "I don't know."

"You are fucking the one killer boy and do not know anything?" Claude snorts in disbelief. "You Americans always think I am a fool. You cannot be entwined with someone and not know the dealings that they are doing. Not when the man looks at you the way he does, not when he has had his brothers protecting you so that we cannot get you." He lifts the scalpel and waves it around in the air, my blood tingeing the blade. "It does not matter. I will get information another way."

And then he brings the scalpel back down to cut across my stomach. The scream that shatters out of me vibrates my bones, and Claude's smile is the cruelest I've ever seen. I close my eyes to try and will the pain away, but Claude reaches up to smack my cheek, bringing me back to reality.

The pain of the cut hurts in a different way than I've ever experienced. This is real pain, the kind that awakens all those primordial feelings inside me to flee, to protect myself, to do anything to stay alive. I tilt my head a little to look at the smashed phone on the ground beside me. Maybe Dante had a brief moment to look at his phone, found the app, and tracked me before it was crushed. Everything I've been doing for the past few years seems so stupid in the grand scheme of everything. All the pain I've caused Mason when we've been through enough pain.

Claude slashes across my stomach again, this time leaning down to hover in my face so I can't disassociate from the moment.

"You know, you did some very bad things with some very bad men before entangling yourself with these stupid little boys," Claude says carefully, eyes shrewd and angry. "Did you know you were fucking the biggest drug kingpin in Eastport?"

"I never do repeats," I say through clenched teeth.

Claude tilts his head while slashing the knife across my stomach again. "Even when you took the drugs you bought from them?"

Oh, I don't want to think about that. All the stupid shit I've done. The mistakes I've made.

"I was brought here to punish you for those boys killing the king, but I am here for my own ends. Yes, they pay me a lot, but I am here for my own purpose. It is more interesting to me what they do than the fact you like to let any person with a dick come inside you."

My nostrils flare as I stare up at him. "I liked you a little, until you got mean."

"You thought a man nicknamed The Carver would be nice? Simpleton."

"Less talking, more cutting," I spit at him.

Claude grins. "Okay. What is the name of their leader?"

I stare up at him, all vitriol and fury. Nothing he does will get a word out of me. He'll kill me anyway. What's the point? Claude stands, visibly frustrated with my lack of snitching, and pulls a bottle of rubbing alcohol out of his pants pocket. I watch detachedly as he twists the cap, then slowly tips it over with a grin. Pain explodes through me and I scream again as my wounds sizzle and burn. At least they're clean now. Maybe I won't get tetanus and die, if I can live through this.

Claude grins wickedly, pulls a cell phone out of his pocket, and disappears toward the back of the room while speaking quick Russian. Shivers of pain and adrenaline rack through me. Tilting my head back, I take slow even breaths so that the wounds on my stomach can't be stretched. Birds fly overhead, calling out as they drift higher toward the fractured blue sky. I wonder if Dante has figured anything out yet. Will they come for me? Will I smell him one more time?

I float in and out of awareness as the pain reaches a crescendo.

Claude reappears with a smile, scalpel dangling from his fingers, and I scream again solely out of fear. His smile grows at the sound.

11

DANTE

The house has been eerily quiet for twelve hours now. Morning came and went. Sunshine peeks in through the back door, but I can't bring myself to care. Reid has been gone for twelve hours. No hint of where he's been taken. Nothing.

I swipe through the photos on my phone to feel an ounce of serotonin. There is one single photo of us together in my entire camera roll. A single photo. Reid is sleeping soundly against my side, his lips pushed up in a pout where his cheek presses against my shoulder. If I close my eyes, I can almost smell his sweet scent, the faint lingering of smoke that clings to his hair after a smoke. I can't sit here and wait anymore. I'm going to go mad with terror and grief.

Swiping through my phone, I notice an app that I never installed hidden away on the last page of my app folders. The icon is black, with a dark green bullseye. When I tap the icon, it requires my facial ID to open.

My phone vibrates softly, before a screen similar to that of a submarine tracking device comes up, revealing a single dot flashing on the screen. I lean forward toward the phone until my face is only inches away.

Location: Eastport steel yard, twelve miles from current location

Holy fuck. I stand so quickly that the chair behind me tips over and crashes to the ground. Mason stands abruptly from the chair he'd been curled up in reading one of Parker's books. Said book falls to the floor as Mason comes toward me, Parker not far behind. My chest is heaving as I stare down in amazement at my phone. Reid—that little shit. He installed software on my phone to track me, but it also tracks him back. Fuck.

"I know where Reid is," I say, suddenly out of breath.

Mason's dark blue eyes widen and his fingers clutch at his arms. "Where?"

"The steel yard," I admit quietly.

Parker swears before disappearing up the stairs to no doubt grab Jacob and Hayden. Just as I'm reaching down to grab the phone, the dot disappears from the screen.

Location: lost

No fucking way. The boys fly down the stairs to surround me in the dining room. I lift my phone and wave it at them, suddenly frantic at what the lost signal could mean.

"Reid must've installed a tracker on our phones. It showed him at the steel yard, but a moment ago it disappeared. It's gone... what if.... Oh my God, Reid."

I fly out the front door, shoeless, and jacketless in the freezing morning air. A shout from behind me roots me to the spot as I rapidly look up and down the street. Where the hell is my bike?

"Put your goddamn shoes and jacket on, Dante. You think you're going to save him without any weapons? Jesus Christ,"

Hayden swears from the front stoop, arms raised in frustration. He points at the stoop while glaring at me. "Get back here. I feel like a fucking mom right now."

I guess he is right. I can't save Reid without weapons. Hayden helps me put on my shoes, then lovingly slides my harness over my shoulders. His hands are trembling slightly as he pats my guns in place. When his gaze lifts to mine, Hayden's eyes are sure and hard.

"We are going to get him back," Hayden promises.

"Did you talk to Robin?" I ask quietly.

Hayden swallows loudly and glances away. "They just told me to do whatever I needed to get Reid back, clean the scene, and they'll worry about the rest."

"Permission to kill?"

Hayden nods. "Everyone."

And that brings a real smile to my face.

We're all finishing getting ready while Mason shifts awkwardly onto his feet. Parker looks over at him with a bemused, fond sort of look, before quickly shaking his head as if scared of himself.

"I don't want to stay here alone... what if they come for me next?" Mason asks timidly.

"You're coming with us," Parker says with finality.

Jacob and Hayden glance at each other, but shrug in acceptance of Parker's decision. We all load into the car together, with Mason sitting in the front so that no one accidentally touches him. After the whole medicine debacle yesterday, it's pretty obvious he has some touching issues. Combined with the nose tap that he and Reid do, it's probably gone on for a very long time.

The ride to the steel yard is quiet. Parker glances in the rearview mirror more than usual, probably to check we aren't being tailed. My heart thrums away in my chest. I can see my heartbeat in my eyes. Jacob leans hard against my shoulder, bringing me back to reality when my thoughts start to shift to all the awful what-ifs that ran through my mind last night. Reid is going to be fine, I say over and over in my head. My new mantra. Maybe I can will it into being true. The universe owes me at least that.

Parker parks the SUV a few blocks from the steel yard. We don't have the cover of night to hide us, but we have guns, and Jacob which is almost just as good. Jacob leans forward in the seat to aim his hard gaze through the windshield. His eyes trail over the barbed fence, the security guard booth, and the gate that locks access to the yard. Containers dot the horizon as far as the eye can see. The stench of trash filters in through the air vents, which will no doubt double once we step out of the car.

Mason shifts awkwardly in the front seat. Finally, after what feels like forever, Jacob leans back and points toward the east side of the yard.

"Cameras won't see that spot there," Jacob points out with perfect confidence. "We can slip in, then pick our way through the containers. Let me lead so I can spot the security weaknesses."

Jacob opens the car door, and holds his hand out for Hayden. Their fingers tangle for a brief moment, before Hayden drops Jacob's hand like he's been burned the moment he's safely outside. I climb out, feeling an odd sense of finality to the moment. Either I bring Reid home, or I do something so drastic even Robin can't clean the scene or keep me out of jail. Parker comes around to Mason's side of the car, and opens his door. Parker's fingers turn white where he grips the metal, eyes firmly on the man sitting safely inside the vehicle.

"Get in the back seat, lie down, keep the car locked no matter what you hear." Parker holds the keys out to Mason and waits for Mason to hesitantly take them in his hand. Once Mason is safely ensconced in the back seat, Parker slams the door shut, and tilts his head in wait for Mason to lock it.

The car door locks and Parker breathes a heavy sigh of relief. We all follow behind Jacob as he leads us toward the fence's vulnerable spot. Keeping one hand on a gun, I follow behind Jacob to slip through the sliver of space between the fence posts. The sun beams over us, but my skin is chilled from the cold air. The scent of metal and sewage lingers over the steel yard, bad enough to make me bite down the urge to gag. I will not puke before the mission has even really begun.

Jacob pads softly along the metal containers, urging us to turn at the whim of the security system weak points. He lifts a hand for us to stop when the sound of voices rise above the cry of vultures above us. The voices are speaking in Russian, so I can't understand a word, but Hayden tilts his head like a dog waiting for a treat.

When Hayden breaks the line and heads to the left, Jacob reaches out to grab him but is a second too late. A moment later the sound of two bodies dropping to the ground echoes around us. Hayden returns while carefully slipping his gun back into the holster.

Hayden points straight ahead, mimes something that I don't understand, then squints his eyes at Jacob. They stare each other down for a hard moment until Jacob seemingly gives up. I don't understand these two and I never will. Hayden shifts to be in front now with Jacob close at his back, almost breathing down Hayden's neck. Any other time Hayden would've elbowed him hard enough to steal Jacob's breath, but for some reason he's putting up with the strange behavior now.

After more seemingly endless walking, we come to stop outside a beaten-down-looking warehouse. Hayden dips quickly and we all follow. Lifting up slightly, I spot three men standing around the warehouse, smoking cigarettes and murmuring amongst themselves. Parker sighs loudly to my right, before lifting the rifle strapped to his back. He takes a few seconds to set it up, squints one eye, taps the gun three times, then rapidly pulls the trigger until all three men are dead on the ground.

Hayden's grin is terrifying. "We're so good at this. It's like a video game."

"These are real people," Jacob murmurs while tiredly pinching his nose.

"Bad people," Hayden corrects with an evil little grin.

We all stand and slowly make our way to the warehouse. The metal creaks when Jacob slides the door open, but there's no sound of other people. A scream echoes around us and my blood goes cold, then immediately boils. That's Reid.

Hayden grabs my arm hard, and his eyes implore me to stay calm. But I can't. That's my man crying out in pain. Suddenly an alarm goes off and Jacob swears loudly as he grabs his guns. Five burly men round the corner, freezing in their spots at the sight of us. A scary hush falls over us as enemies take each other in. The men are all older, covered in scars, obviously used to fights of this kind. But what we lack in age, we make up for in fevered training and the thrill of blood on our hands. Parker is the first to draw his gun, aiming his silencer and pulling the trigger before any man can blink an eye.

Chaos erupts when the man falls to the floor dead, bleeding from the perfect bullet-sized wound in the middle of his forehead. Perfect Aim Parker strikes again. One of the men yells and charges for me, and I focus on him instead of my brothers. I don't have time to grab my own gun before he's pummeling into me and we're fighting. His fist connects with my chin and that fucking hurts, pain radiating through me distracts me only for a moment, before I'm getting my own punch in. The noise around me from the other fights is distant, no longer important as I fight for my life.

The guy is bigger than me, not in height, but in weight, so he has more momentum when he aims a punch for my stomach. I dodge him as best I can, but he still makes contact, and Jesus it's been a while since I've been in a fistfight. I lunge for the gun in his holster at the same time he aims an uppercut to my nose. Fuck. I'm going to have the *biggest* nose of all time if it breaks again. Which only makes me think of Reid. My Reid. My hand wraps around the warm metal of the man's gun and I tug away, only for him to rush at me until we're rolling around on the dirty warehouse floor.

Distantly, I can hear Jacob screaming in his own fight, but I can't focus on him right now, I have to focus on me. We tussle for the gun and the man gets it spun around, pulling the trigger. Oh. That fucking *hurts*. I can't care about where that bullet went or the warm ooze of blood I feel on my side, instead I butt the man's head, grinning when it shocks him into falling to the side. Two seconds is all it takes for me to get the gun to his head and pull the trigger.

I lie there for a second, catching my breath, ignoring the pain at my side, then sit up in a rush.

The sound of gunfire echoes around us, blood spraying everywhere as the fights continue. Parker is engaged in hand-to-hand combat with two of the men, while another man has Hayden in a tight headlock while Jacob tries to take him out. Jesus, we're all a mess. A scream rents through the air, not coming from any of us. That's Reid. Fuck. Where the hell is he?

Parker uses the men's momentary distraction at the sound of Reid's scream to do one of his weird karate moves that has them both bonking their heads together, then slumping to the floor like rag dolls. The final man standing now looks agitated and terrified, his grip tightening around Hayden's neck.

Hayden's eyes are calm, arms limp at his side, as his gaze stays firm on Jacob. I can't hear what they're talking about, instead I look down to see blood oozing from beneath my black tactical gear. Fuck. Parker hurries over, presses a hand to my stomach, then his dark brown eyes meet mine. His hair is messy, slightly curly from sweat.

"You need a haircut," I tell like the stupid fuck I am.

Parker bites back a smirk. "I told you, I'm growing it out."

"Awkward length," I mumble in annoyance.

Parker shoots a look over his shoulder, lips curling in distaste as Jacob is still trying to talk the man out of letting Hayden go. Over it all, Parker stands, marches over, pulls his silencer, and shoots the man dead.

Jacob lets out the loudest huff of all time. "We needed *one* of them alive to ask questions."

Hayden yelps and jumps away from the dead man that had been holding him captive. "You were far too comfortable with him possibly killing me," Hayden says as he tugs on his shirt to straighten it out.

"He wasn't going to kill you," Jacob argues.

Hayden stares at him hard. "Oh yeah?"

"I wouldn't have let him," Jacob says with finality.

Silence echoes around us.

Then another scream.

And then I see red.

My speed is unmatched. The boys lag behind me as I run toward the sound of Reid's scream. We're magnets. My body knows the way to Reid before my brain can even fucking catch up. Everything hurts, blood drips down my side, my nose and jaw thrum with the pulse of bruises to come, but none of that matters. All that matters is that I get to Reid.

Claude was right. It *doesn't* feel good when the cutting is not in my control. He leans over me, smelling like rank sweat, and the scalpel draws another thin line along my abdomen. I am not going to give him the satisfaction of crying.

"Are there other groups in other cities?" Claude asks, breath smelling like death.

"I don't *know*," I answer through gritted teeth.

My limbs are shaking from the pain and adrenaline. The feeling of my blood dripping down my sides makes me want to vomit again. Claude makes an exasperated noise as he sits back up, dragging the scalpel again. A scream erupts from me before I can hold it back. Slash after slash, I can't even hear the questions Claude is murmuring to me anymore. He seems to catch on and stands with a disgusted look on his face. My blood drips from the scalpel, and this time the food from earlier does return. Rolling over onto my side, I vomit again, then wince when the wounds on my stomach ache with my skin pulling tight.

"Useless," Claude says angrily. He kicks my back hard. I groan with the ache of the force of his steel-toed boot to my back.

Resting my head against the cold, damp concrete, I pray for death to take me. The sound of gunshots echoes through the room. My skin is clammy with sweat, fear rattling through me. A little more bile rises up in me, but I swallow it down to not anger Claude further. I've really got to get the puking under control. It happens far too much.

Rolling over onto my back, I wince at the pain radiating through me, and watch distantly as Claude walks toward the door with a purposeful, angry stride. Before he can even get out of the door, it swings open to reveal Dante with a gun raised. Claude is big and fast though, grabbing the gun from Dante in a flash. I must make some noise because Dante's eyes flit to me. Fury overtakes his beautiful face at the sight of me bloody and beaten on the ground. My Dante.

"You're a dead man," Dante says from between his teeth.

Claude chuckles, dangling the gun from his pointer finger in a mocking manner. "Children. You've *no* idea what you've done!"

Because Dante has no fear of danger, he lunges for Claude and surprises him with a right hook to the corner of his jaw. There's a tense pause for a moment, before they're locked in a fistfight, the gun lying forgotten on the floor. I try to move over, do something fucking useful, anything, but then the tug of the chain on my arm reminds me that I'm stuck. Fuck.

"There's a balance!" Claude shouts as Dante gets in a good punch to his shoulder. "You kill too many bad people and the world doesn't work right. You are all children! Playing like gods."

"We're *helping* people!" Dante shouts back.

"You're laying waste to an industry!" Claude snarls, spittle flying from his cut lip.

Their limbs move so fast it's hard for me to keep up with who is where. But there's blood oozing from Dante's shirt, fast and dark, and Claude notices because he aims his knee right for that spot. But because Dante is made of steel and anger, the knee to his injury does nothing.

Shit. Where are the boys? Dante gets them to the ground, rolling around in a way that looks extremely painful, and then Dante has the gun back in his hands. Letting out a roar, he aims the gun at Claude's stomach and pulls the trigger. After using the butt of the gun to Claude's head, effectively knocking him out, Dante flops over onto the ground.

I think I died under Claude's torture and I'm dreaming about Dante saving me. What a beautiful dream.

"Dante!" I cry out, voice hoarse to my own ears.

Dante's eyes find me just as he lifts to his knees on the cold concrete.

Blood is everywhere. I don't know if it's mine, Dante's, or one of the men he laid waste to as he came to save me. Jesus. I crawl across the floor, body shaking the closer I get to him. But I can't go any further because of the chains. Dante coughs, then tries to grab at a wound on his side. Fuck. He crawls closer, just close enough for me to reach.

"Dante, baby." I rest my bloody hand on his cheek once I'm close enough to touch him.

Dante's eyes flutter open, but they're almost lifeless, not dark with want like usual. A bittersweet smile tilts his lips up at the sight of me.

"Reid. Sweetheart."

I choke back an anguished cry. I brush the matted hair

from his face, then dip down to kiss him softly on the mouth. He tastes like the metallic tang of blood but I don't fucking care. My hand trembles where it combs through his hair and his breaths are coming quieter as he stares up at me like I'm the answer to the universe. I need to save him. Need to keep him. He's mine forever.

"Dante," I whisper brokenly.

"Mmm. Luv way you say m'name," Dante slurs. "Luv... you..."

I can feel the tears sliding down my bloody cheeks, and this isn't the way Dante likes to make me cry. This isn't right. I lean my forehead against his, hoping maybe I can share my breath with him long enough to make him be okay. Make this all okay. A shout from outside the door tries to grab my attention but I can't pull my focus from Dante. He's my entire world. All that matters anymore is Dante.

"Fuck, that's a lot of blood," Parker cries out from the door.

"Help him!" I scream, feeling the adrenaline start to flee my body.

After a few seconds getting my chains undone, Jacob picks me up from the floor as Hayden and Parker carefully lift Dante from the ground. The bodies that litter the room are ignored as we make a hasty retreat. The sunlight hurts my eyes, but I don't have the energy to lift my hand to shield them. I watch as Dante is loaded into the back of the SUV, lying flat in the back. Parker sets me up front, but I immediately turn around to watch Dante.

"Give me his hand," I demand without a shit in the world.

Someone places Dante's hand in mine. It's Mason, he's in the back with Dante, covered in blood, but not caring for the first time in his life. I rest my head against the console, holding tightly to Dante's hand as we navigate the roads to go wherever we need to go to save him. His heartbeat is weak under my thumb. If Dante dies, I'm going to die too. I won't survive losing him. Dante's the only good thing in my life, the only thing worth living for, and the only bit of danger I can stomach anymore. Life without Dante would be meaningless and devoid of all joy. He's... he's it. He's mine. The sun in the bleak pitch-blackness of my perpetually dark life.

We pass by one of those fancy-ass hotels downtown, turning into the basement where workers probably park. The basement is devoid of cars and people, only Mandy from the diner stands outside the door to the bowels of the hotel. What the fuck? Parker helps me out of the car, but I push him away. I'm not letting go of Dante. Once they've got him out of the vehicle, I limp behind them with Dante's hand still in my grip.

Mandy opens the door leading inside and frantically ushers us in with a quick wave of her hand. Oh. This all makes a lot more sense now. We follow her into the long fluorescent hallways, and she leads us deeper into the oddly quiet hotel basement. Turning into a brightly lit, sterile room, there's a medical table set up. I watch as the boys lift Dante onto it, his blood-soaked clothes immediately dyeing the white paper crimson. Fuck he's lost so much blood. My head wooshes at the sight, dizziness threatening to sweep me under its tide. I'm so scared for Dante that my vision is starting to go black, my wobbly knees threatening to crumble me to the ground.

"Where's it coming from," Mandy murmurs while hastily stripping away Dante's blood-sodden clothes. Shivers of fear roll through me, only getting worse when they find the source of the blood at a deep wound on his abdomen, another on his thigh. I blink slowly and suddenly I'm on a table beside him. I blink again and they're all looming over me, blurry in my distorted vision.

I blink again and Dante's clammy hand is no longer in mine.

Another slow blink.

Tilting my head to the side I steal one last look of Dante, finding his glassy eyes already staring back at me. When I reach my hand out, our fingers just barely graze before the last blink steals me away.

———

Beep. Beep. Beep.

Oh my God, my head hurts something fierce. Worse than when I take one of those random pills at the club. Deja vu. Also, my mouth tastes like ass—not in a good way—and it's dry as fuck. It takes every ounce of energy to blink my dry, crusty eyes open. Someone gasps sharply and then Mason is leaning over me, eyes red-rimmed from crying, and bottom lip caught between his teeth.

"Jesus, Reid." Mason reaches a shaky hand out to touch me, but retracts it quickly. After taking a deep breath, he reaches out to softly touch my hand where it lies over the fluffy white blanket. "You scared the shit out of me."

"What happened?"

Mason's breath trembles. "You lost a lot of blood, we didn't realize how bad your cuts were until you passed out beside Dante. I donated some to you, we're the same blood type."

I blink slowly at him. "Will I be afraid of germs now too?"

Mason's face is stoic for one long moment, before he erupts into relieved laughter. "No, Reid."

His hand is warm over mine, so I flip my hand over to tangle our fingers together. I don't think I've touched Mason's skin since we were children, since before his childhood cancer.

"I'm sorry to scare you."

Mason's smile is so warm. "Hush, you're okay now."

"I'm thirsty."

Mason bends to the side to grab a Styrofoam cup off the table by my bed. The room I'm in doesn't seem to be a hospital room, instead decorated like an upscale hotel room. All the memories from the past few days come rushing back, making me gasp as my free hand flies to my stomach. I wince when I press too hard, flaring the tenderness of my wounds. Mason shushes me again and raises the cup to my lips so I can take a sip from the straw.

"Where's Dante?" I ask once I've decimated the cup of water.

"In the room next door," Mason replies quickly. "He's okay."

"I need to see him... take me to him. Please."

Mason looks like he's going to argue with me for a long moment, until giving in at whatever look he sees on my face. It takes a while to get me sitting up, the wounds on my abdomen still tender and covered in bandages. We shuffle toward the door that must connect our bedrooms with Mason carefully dragging along the IV stand beside me. Mason knocks on the door and it's opened a second later by a worried-looking Parker. But he doesn't clock me first, instead his gaze falls on Mason, relief washing over him when he finds Mason okay. I don't know what that's about, don't really care right now, I just have to get to Dante.

Parker takes over for Mason to help me shuffle toward the bed. Dante lies so still, face so pale, tattoos a stark color against his skin. Without asking, without hesitation, I climb into the empty side of the bed. I curl up on my side, close enough to hopefully bleed some of my warmth into him. The IV painfully tugs at my arm as I sift my fingers through Dante's dirty curls, fingers catching on the strands caked with his blood.

"Dante, come back to me," I whisper against his ear. "I love you too, you fucking asshole."

"Yeah?" comes a quiet voice.

I freeze. Lifting up slightly onto my elbow, I look down at a very clearly awake Dante.

"You fucking asshole!"

His hand reaches out to grab my wrist, tugging me down until my chest is pressed against his arm, but my stomach isn't touching him anywhere. Dante stares at me for one long moment, eyelashes fanning across his cheek with each slow blink.

"Say it again," Dante orders tiredly.

"You fucking asshole?"

Dante suddenly looks very exhausted. "No, you know what I want."

"I love you, jerk."

"Come here." Dante tugs me closer until he can kiss me softly, his eyes closed tight while I watch his eyes crinkle with love just from our kiss. "Be a good boy and take a nap with me."

"You guys just slept for twelve hours," Jacob groans from across the room.

Dante hums in indifference. "Fuck off. We're alive. Wake us up in a few more hours."

I keep my eyes on Dante as the sounds of people leaving the room reaches me. Once we're alone, I press my forehead to Dante's, breathing him in despite the smell of sweat and the metallic tang of blood.

"You saved me," I murmur against the shadow of a beard on his chin.

"Can't let anyone else hurt you, huh? Only I get to make you cry."

I don't laugh, don't argue. Instead, I lie back down beside him, head tucked against his bicep, his hand hot on the small of my back. Despite not being very sleepy, I fall asleep fast in the comfort of Dante's arms.

———

THE NEXT TIME I wake up, it's to Dante's hands gently carding through my hair. That feeling when you nap too long during the day, when you wake up sweaty, disoriented, and like you've missed a few years, washes over me. I press tighter against Dante, hissing when pain flares through my abdomen. Ugh.

"We're both fucked up," Dante says with a gentle laugh.

"In many ways," I agree.

He hums gently, but keeps sifting through my hair, making me want to purr and push closer despite the pain both of our bodies are steeped in. The urge to pee takes precedence though. When I swing my legs over the edge of the bed, the door opens quickly to reveal a harried-looking Jacob.

"Wait, Jesus Christ." Then his strong hands are there to help me up.

We shuffle awkwardly to the bathroom. The IV is gone now, so it must've been removed while I slept beside Dante. It's the longest piss of my life, and I usually count, so I'd definitely know. Once done, Jacob gently holds my elbow while I wash my hands and look longingly at the shower.

"Not for a few more days. Doctor's orders. Sponge baths only," Jacob reprimands as if I'm a child.

I wiggle my eyebrows at him. "Are you volunteering?"

Jacob visibly retches. "No."

Alright, then. Once I'm back in the bed, Jacob repeats the process with Dante. It would be comical watching Dante, who looms over Jacob, be helped to the bathroom, if it wasn't for the clear pain on Dante's face. They bicker back and forth in the bathroom because Dante probably isn't any better than me when it comes to being helped, then they're shuffling back toward the bed. Dante lies down beside me with a relieved sigh.

Jacob slaps his hands together and promptly disappears back into the other room. A second later the boys and my still harried-looking brother join us in our room. I don't have the energy to care about how I look, not when my body feels like it's been sliced like a deli ham. I curl against Dante, letting the warmth of his palm against my hip steady me.

"So, that was crazy," Jacob says with a whistle.

"And our only lead is dead," Parker notes wryly.

Hayden chuckles darkly. "Look, Reid, you've got to tell us what the big Russian told you."

"He just kept asking who you guys answered to," I tell them honestly, wrung out and tired. "Wanted to know what I knew... why I meant something to you."

Dante's hand squeezes my hip tight. "I'll kill him."

"Settle down, big guy. I'm here now." I smile against Dante's chest when his fingers dip down to possessively curve over my ass. "He didn't seem *that* excited to be torturing me."

I lift my head to watch Hayden sit down on the corner of the bed as he flicks through an iPad. He flips it over to show me a picture of Claude, maybe a little younger, but it's definitely the same guy that spent a few hours making my life hell the other day.

"The Carver," Hayden supplies as the other boys look over his shoulder. "Russian hired killer for more people than I can count. He was expensive, so whoever hired him definitely wanted to know whatever it is that you know."

"But I don't know anything and that's what I told him."

"That's not true," Parker argues, eyebrows furrowed. "You know we answer to Robin. You know we steal from the evil to give back to those that deserve it."

I shrug and lift my head to rest it over Dante's chest. "Didn't need to tell him that. He seemed to already know."

"Oh?" Hayden says, blinking quickly.

"Hmmm. He knew. He just wanted to know if there were *more* of you. He said the local drug kingpin hired him, but he was there for his own answers." I shrug as well as I can despite the pain. "He was getting paid to fuck with me, but wanted answers for himself."

Hayden stands quickly from the bed, looking stricken. "What?"

"Yeah," I say through a yawn. "He kept asking if I knew about the others. What cities you were all in and how you communicated. I told him the hell if I know, I'm not part of the group."

Jacob snorts. "Well, kid, you are now whether you want to

be or not." Jacob aims a sidelong glance at Mason who's wringing his hands while we all talk. "So's your brother. Better safe in the circle than dead on the outside."

Mason visibly blanches, face paling. "Great!"

"Mason," I say softly, lifting my head up until our gazes meet. "I'm fine. We're going to be fine."

The main door to the hotel slowly opens to reveal a silver fox and Mandy. I was so out of it from surviving and telling Dante that I loved him that I hadn't even put any thought into *how* we survived. Mandy pushes past the man to hurry toward my side of the bed. That feels wrong. Shouldn't she go to Dante first.

Her hands brush my hair back as she takes me in, eyes flitting over my face almost to ensure I'm still alive. This is weird. My face must echo my thoughts because she pulls away with a slightly harried chuckle.

"Sorry. Your injuries were just so bad... it's so nice to see you up and awake."

"Okay," I say because I don't know what else to fucking say.

"Hello? What am I? Chopped liver?" Dante grumbles as he takes in the scene in front of him.

Mandy rolls her eyes. "You're fine, you big lug."

"She likes my boyfriend more than me," Dante complains, fingers pressing tighter against my thigh.

Mandy backs away to join the smirking doctor at the edge of the bed.

"Mandy can normally handle the smaller injuries on her own, but she called me in when she realized Dante had an entrance wound for the bullet, but no exit. So, this guy got surgery to remove the bullet." The doctor stares Dante down, hard, making me squirm a little on the bed. But Dante is unmoving because he's Dante. "You are on bedrest for weeks. You've got twenty-five stitches, you're at risk for internal bleeding, and your boyfriend here is almost just as bad."

I gasp dramatically. "I had a gunshot wound?"

Mason sighs deeply. "Reid."

"No, but you have almost as many stitches and you lost enough blood to need a transfusion from your very kind brother over here."

"What's your name so I can stop calling you *the doctor* in my head when you say something that pisses me off?" I ask with a sneer. Dante's hand tightens on my hip, so I soften my sneer, making it an unpleasant grimace instead.

"Eric."

"Thank you, Eric," Dante says without any malice. "We'd have been dead if you didn't help Mandy take care of us. So, thank you."

Eric waves us away. "I owe Mandy many favors. But doing surgery in the basement of the hotel I own was not how I wanted to spend my Saturday morning. So you can send thank-you cards to Mandy. Also, you're due for a check-up of your wounds in a few weeks. Stitches should dissolve on their own, but still we want to make sure you healed correctly."

"Thank you," all of the boys echo in the back like a bunch of Boy Scouts.

"I've left your care notes with that one," Eric says while pointing at a very responsible-looking Jacob. "But my phone number is at the bottom of the sheet in case there are any other questions. Antibiotics for a few days to prevent infections, pain pills if needed, and your IVs have been removed, so, I think Mandy can handle it from here."

Eric flees the hotel room like a hound out of hell. I get it. I wouldn't want to be in this room either if I was given an option. I cuddle back to Dante, enjoying his warmth, already wanting to go back the fuck to sleep. Jesus. Nothing like almost losing your life to realize just how amazing sleep is, especially when pressed against the man that killed for you.

Hayden makes an odd noise as he reads his phone, all the boys turning to look at him.

"Robin just informed me about cleanup... Claude wasn't there," Hayden announces, voice light like he's out of breath. "Just a pool of blood and nothing else."

"What?" Parker asks in disbelief.

Hayden lifts his head to stare at Jacob, lip caught between his teeth. "Looks like Dante didn't kill our only lead."

"Or we are now also facing a zombie epidemic," Dante says with a laugh. Nobody else laughs though. Despite the fraught nature of the moment, sleep is coming for me again, the dark tendrils tugging me down.

Finally, sleep comes for me as the murmur of voices at the end of the bed floats in and out. Dante pets my hair, murmurs words into my neck, and I fall asleep held in his arms, safe and loved, and for the first time in my life, I believe it. To be loved. It's kind of nice.

WE ENDED up in the hotel for almost a week until Dante and I grew restless enough to piss them all off enough to take us back home. The wounds on my abdomen are still bandaged, needing cleaning and cream put on them at the end of each day. Oddly, when I look at them now, it makes all the times I used to do it to myself seem pretty stupid. I'll work through that in therapy, I guess. When I go. Which I probably should.

Dante is another story. The man likes to act like he's a god himself, if he just walks off the bullet wounds, then he'll be fine. I've had to resort to bribery to keep him from overdoing himself which usually results in lazy blow jobs and dirty talk. By the time we're both healed enough to return to daily life, two weeks have passed by.

And I haven't slept in my own bed in just that long.

I don't know if I can sleep away from Dante anymore.

Don't know if I can go back to *normal* life.

But it also doesn't help that I'm not allowed to go anywhere alone anymore.

I'm getting dressed for school in Dante's walk-in closet when Dante swaggers in, sweatpants low on his hips, bandages still covering the almost healed wounds on his side and thigh. It's kind of sexy in a devil-may-care sort of way. But I'm afraid that everything about Dante is sexy to me. Even when he snores after a long day.

"I got you something," Dante says with a sly little smile.

"I told you, I'm not wearing a collar."

Dante stares blankly back at me. "We never discussed that."

Sigh. "What is it?"

I shove my feet into my boots, staring down at the floor as I do so, but glance up when Dante stays quiet. In the palm of his hand is a very obvious red velvet box. My heart thumps heavily in my chest, vision going a little blurry. But Dante's grin is warm as usual, even just a little mean, no doubt enjoying my terrified reaction to the box.

"Calm down," Dante teases. He opens the box to reveal a sleek black ring. Grabbing my hand, he slides the ring onto my middle finger, and that's when I notice light-blue-looking gemstones blinking up at me. "It's a tracker. In case you lose your phone."

I squint my eyes at him. "What about you? If you get to track me, then—"

"Already done," Dante interrupts me, lifting up his hand to show a matching ring on his own middle finger. "Quid pro quo."

"Oh, you feel fancy now that you know that saying but I was using it in the context of sex, which was a little more fun."

"Being able to track my every movement isn't fun?"

I flush a little because yes it is, but well... "The hunt was fun too."

Dante's grin warms me to the core, and my insides squirm when he leans down a little to be close to my face. "We can still play cat and mouse sometimes, pretend like we can't track each other."

"Okay," I whisper excitedly.

Dante looks pleased just before dipping down to kiss me soft and slow. Tangling my fingers in his shirt, I tug him closer, careful of his still healing wounds. We haven't fucked for ages and I miss it, but an hour before class isn't the time. Dante's hands drift down to my ass, squeeze hard, then go to lift in the telltale sign of him wanting to pick me up.

I slap his chest and pull away from his mouth. "Nope. You're not going to open those stitches up because you want to fuck me against the wall. Save it."

Dante groans in obvious annoyance, but doesn't argue. He goes back to lie on the bed, leaned back on his elbows, eyes heavy as he watches me finish getting dressed. I stop by the bed, fitting myself between his splayed thighs, and lean down to kiss him with my eyes open. He lifts his hand to curl his fingers around my ear, quickly angling my head so that he can lick into my mouth at exactly the angle he wants.

When I pull away to straighten my clothes and jacket, Dante squints his eyes at me critically.

"Are you going to dye your hair soon?" Dante asks.

I smile down at him. "Maybe I'll do something different."

Dante thumps back down on the bed. "Sexy no matter what."

"I know."

When I walk into the kitchen, Hayden is at the table with his laptop while Jacob cooks breakfast. I slide into the chair across from Hayden with a soft clearing of my throat. A moment later, a plate of food appears before me like I've summoned it through magic. I blink my eyes coyly up at Jacob and he flicks my cheek with his finger, making me scowl at his back as he fixes Hayden a plate.

Hayden spins his computer around and shoves it toward me. "Help me with this line of code, please."

I pick at the protein waffles as I peck at the keys on Hayden's computer. It's a simple fix, and when I slide the computer back toward him, he grunts in acceptance of my greater knowledge. Dante slips down in the chair beside me, then leans over to press a kiss to my cheek.

The sound of the front door slamming open has me looking over my shoulder to find Parker wandering in.

"Snowing!" Parker calls out while taking off his shoes.

"Fuck, I have class in fifteen minutes," Jacob whines.

Hayden stands and makes his way to the kitchen, hip-checks Jacob away from the sink. "I'll do the dishes for you."

"You do the dishes *badly*," Jacob points out, but doesn't move to stop Hayden. They have some wordless exchange until Jacob huffs, then disappears toward the front door to leave for class.

The house is warm, my stomach is full, and Dante's hand

is a brand on my thigh under the table. I lean my elbow against the table, softly putting my chin in the palm of my hand to watch Dante eat.

He chews on his waffle while turning to face me. "What?"

I didn't expect to find an odd sort of little family when I stalked Dante all those months ago. Didn't expect to fall into this Avengers type of plot either. But it's nice to have something like a family for once, people that choose me, people that keep an eye out for me.

"I think I'll move in permanently," I tell Dante, grinning when his eyes bug out.

"Really?"

"Yeah, why not?"

"What about Mason?" Dante asks, eyebrows furrowed.

I glance over toward Parker in the living room where he's standing still, distractedly removing his scarf from around his neck. He stares down at his phone with a shy little smile on his face, and somehow I know exactly why he's smiling, and who exactly put that smile there.

"I'm not worried about Mason at all anymore."

13

DANTE

Finally, my stitches are out and I'm all healed. I skip out of the doctor's office feeling like a free fucking man. Am I excited to be cleared? Yes. But I am more excited to see Reid because he promised all sorts of vile and despicable things once I finally got permission from the doctor. I even got a nice little doctor's note clearing me for *all* physical activities.

Parker idles at the curb waiting for me since it's snowing again, which means no motorcycle. I shake off the snow from my jacket once I'm in the heated passenger seat. It's so fucking cold. I miss summer and spring.

"So?" Parker asks while navigating out of the parking lot.

"All clear!"

"Nice, now you can get back to work."

"Now I can fuck my boyfriend," I clarify.

Parker rolls his eyes. "Getting back to work is more important."

"Let's agree to disagree." I tap my fingers on my jean-clad thighs for a few moments, too anxious to sit still. Good time to bother Parker. "How's it going with Mason?"

Parker cuts me a look so vile that I fight the urge to squirm. "I'm keeping him safe, that's it. I'm straight."

"Sure."

"I am!"

"Absolutely."

"Dante."

"Oh my God, fuck off. I don't really care. Just that's Reid's brother, so don't be a total asshole, okay, or I'll have to do something very serious.... to you."

Parker snorts. "I'm not afraid of you. Big baddie with a heart of gold."

"I have a higher kill count than you."

"That you know of."

Parker slams the car into park the moment we pull into the garage, jumping out to head inside before I can even think of how to parse apart his answer. The house is quiet when I step inside. Darkness falls over the kitchen from the heavy snow falling past the windows. A plate of brownies sits in the middle of the dining table, and I grab two as I head off to locate Reid.

Finding Reid is easy these days. He's sitting by the fire in the living room, curled up in the chair that Hayden bought for him since the couch is usually taken up by the four of us. He looks so small in the chair, smaller than normal, his small feet tucked up under his thighs. He's got his sketchbook balanced on his thighs, lip caught between his teeth in thought. How this man is mine will always amaze me. I drop to my knees in front of him, handing him a brownie with a smile only ever meant for him.

"I've had one already," Reid murmurs, nose wrinkled in disdain.

"You can have another."

Reid sniffs, but doesn't argue. He lets me feed him bites of the brownie as he continues to draw. Feeding him is something we've found that we both like, even when it's not my cock. Something about taking care of Reid lights up all those fun receptors in my brain, the same ones that find joy in making him cry, in making him hurt. I don't want to think too much about it.

"What are you drawing?" I ask, leaning over to try to sneak a peek.

Reid tilts his sketchpad up with a scowl. "Excuse you."

I wiggle my eyebrows. "I can make you show me."

"Likely story."

I rise to my knees and loom over him, tucking my head into the crook of his neck to kiss the rapid beat of his pulse. His breath catches in his chest, sketchbook falling to his lap as his fingers come up to tangle in my hair. Moving his shirt out of the way, I bite the tender, meaty part of his shoulder, and he hisses in pleasure at the feeling of my teeth against his skin. When I pull away, his eyes are blown and I can't help but lean down to kiss his plush lips. He opens up for me like always, eager and wanting.

"Excuse me," Hayden calls out from behind us.

Reid drops his hands from my hair like he was burned. Clearing his throat, Reid's eyes dip down to the sketchbook in his lap, tugging it against his chest before I can sneak a look.

Hayden comes to stand beside us, hand held out with a thin letter dangling between his fingers. "This came for you."

Reid takes the envelope with a confused look, eyes tracking Hayden as he disappears up the stairs, Jacob hot on his heels. Reid spins the envelope in his fingers a few times, then gazes up at me with a million questions in his eyes. I shrug because I have no idea what it is either. I stand quickly, picking Reid up despite his squawk of annoyance, then toss myself back to settle him in my lap.

Reid raises one eyebrow. "I assume the doctor went well?"

"Yes, all clear." I squeeze his hip hard. "We can talk about that later though. What's in the envelope?"

I will never be able to explain why it turns me on when Reid delicately uses his finger to open the flap of the envelope. He peers inside for a moment, hair falling into his eyes, then shakes his hair away as he tugs the piece of paper out. His eyes scan over the paper, squinting in confusion, then crimson dots across his cheeks. Whatever is in the letter made him happy.

"Did you do this?" Reid asks, voice tinged with awe.

"Do what?" I lean closer to read the letter hanging precariously in his hand.

REID

THANK you for keeping my secrets. In exchange for your helpfulness, I've had the CEO of FlyNow killed. By the time you read this letter, he'll be lying in a pile of his own vomit, appearing to have died from an overdose. Nasty things those painkillers are.

I'D ALSO like you to consider becoming one of my boys. Hayden reports that you're very savvy with hacking and coding, which can be useful so that I can utilize Hayden in other ways. Your parents' killer being put down should not sway you, make the decision with your heart so that you can have a clean conscience like the other boys.

. . .

Please give Hayden your answer.

Keep Dante safe, he's very important to me.

What.

I stare down at the letter a few times before lifting my gaze to look at Reid. His eyes are already firmly on me, flicking over my face as if trying to memorize the moment.

"Did you know about this?" Reid asks breathlessly.

"No? Only Hayden communicates with Robin."

"No... killing the CEO. Did you do it?"

"No..." I say slowly. "But I wish I had thought of it first."

"You'd have killed him for me?"

"Reid, I killed men to save you just a few weeks ago, what would one more be to me?"

Reid makes a sort of broken sound before surging up to kiss me. I stand from the chair in a smooth motion, laughing against Reid's mouth when he squawks and scrambles to keep the sketchbook from falling to the floor. Plundering his mouth as we climb the stairs to my room, his cock is hard as granite against my stomach. Jesus. He gets so hard at the idea of me killing for him, almost as hard as he gets when I make him cry.

Kicking my room door open, I shove it closed behind us with the heel of my shoe. Reid kisses me passionately, as if he's starving for me, as if I'm all he needs to live. Maybe I am. I set him down carefully on the ground, holding his shoulders when he sways closer to me. With the tips of my fingers,

I shove him against the door, pointedly saying, "Stay," as I back up towards the bed. The sketchbook falls to the floor when Reid presses his hands flat against the wood of the door.

I sit down carefully, kick off my shoes, then lean back on the bed. I let my gaze sweep over Reid because I know he'll like it. The flush on his throat that works down under my T-shirt that he borrowed when he woke up. The darkness of his pupils even in the almost pitch black of the bedroom.

Snapping my fingers between my thighs, I say, "Crawl to me."

Reid mewls in pleasure before dropping hard enough to his knees that I worry he'll be in pain tomorrow. He crawls to me slowly on all fours, head held high so his gaze can stay locked on mine. It's the most beautiful sight I've ever seen, Reid on his knees for me. The dynamic between us is ever changing, ever growing, but there's a deep pleasure in knowing what Reid needs and giving it to him because it's always exactly what I need. Our needs always perfectly aligned.

"Stop."

Reid stops in his crawling, eyes locked on me.

"Grab the sketchbook," I order.

Reid looks like he's going to argue for one moment, before shifting to his knees and bending backwards to grab the offending object. He shuffles closer on his knees so that he can hold the sketchbook out to me.

"Good boy."

Reid shivers at the praise. He licks his lips. "Don't good boys get rewards?"

"Sometimes," I reply, flipping through the sketchbook to the page he was working on. It's us tangled in bed, Reid's hands holding on to the headboard as I hitch one of his legs up to slide inside him. Dirty as sin to know he drew this while daydreaming about it.

Flipping to the previous page, my heart skips two beats. Reid lunges forward to grab it from me, but I stop him with a hand to his chest. Why didn't he want me to see this one? It's us curled around each other, clothed, contented smiles on our faces. I remember this moment. It was a week ago when Reid' bandages had come off, when I'd rubbed his abdomen with a loving smile while kissing him breathless. He'd fallen asleep in my arms afterwards, pliant and pleased.

"Why don't you show me these kinds of drawings?" I ask curiously.

Reid squeezes his eyes shut tight. "You already know... how I feel. I don't have to show you all the time, do I?"

"I guess not, but you could."

"Can't I just suck your dick?"

I hum and toss the sketchbook aside, plans forgotten. "Change of plans."

Reid groans in frustration. I tug him up onto the bed, kissing him to stop all his arguments. Once he's soft in my hands, I slide my hands under the baggy T-shirt, wanting to feel the familiar scars that are just as much a part of him as my scars are to me now. Reid's breath catches for a moment, before stuttering out in a rush as I tug the shirt over his head.

"Hey, Reid?"

"What?" Reid asks in frustration as I kiss down his chest.

Leaning my chin against his stomach, I smile up at him. "I'd kill anyone you'd ask me to. Kill a hundred million times for you. All you ever have to do is ask."

"Oh, Jesus."

And then I take him apart with my mouth until he's

screaming, begging me to let him come, thighs trembling around my head. I only let him come after edging him for hours, blissed out on the thought of only me ever getting to give him this gift. When Reid finally comes, he's starry-eyed and moldable under my hands when I pull him against the line of my body. I situate the covers over us, kissing his damp temple.

————

THE BED IS empty when I wake up in the middle of the night. Fear grips me tight, but my phone is silent which means Reid is still somewhere in the house with his tracker on. I pull on the shirt and sweatpants that were hastily thrown to the floor hours ago before we made love. The glow of the fire downstairs greets me as I descend the stairs.

Reid is curled up in the chair, chin in his hand, staring at the fire like it contains every single secret of the universe. He doesn't lift his gaze to mine, but his hand falls into my hair when I lower myself to sit by his feet. Taking one of his feet in my lap, I massage the arch until his gaze slides to me.

"I think I'm going to say yes," Reid says, out of the blue.

Ah. "You don't have to, it's your decision."

"I want to," Reid argues, eyebrows furrowing as he stares back at the fire. "Maybe it'll help me get over everything, doing something good, instead of punishing myself for something that isn't even my fault."

"It helped me," I admit.

Reid's worried gaze pings back to me. "Your sister?"

I nod. I watch the glow of the fire move across his face, aching with just how beautiful he is to me. I think I'd love Reid in every universe, no matter how damaged we both are, our souls call out to each other with knowing. Soulmates? Maybe. But his hurt aligns perfectly with mine, somehow making us just one person when we're together.

"I don't know what I'll do after college, not sure this shit is a career, but for now it feels good, and that's what matters most. Right?"

Reid nods in agreement, then leans down to kiss me. When Reid lifts his head, it's to look over my shoulder. When I glance behind me, it's to find a tired-looking Hayden standing in just a pair of sweats, skin dotted with goose pimples from the cold.

"So?" Hayden asks, voice carefully neutral.

"I'll join you," Reid says with a scary smile. "But you'll need to teach me how to use a gun."

I groan in despair at the very thought. But both boys smile at each other, in pleasure at my pain, or pleasure at Reid joining the brotherhood, I'll never know.

EPILOGUE

DANTE

I wake up one Saturday morning to the hazy fall of snow outside my dark windows. Instinctively, I reach over to Reid's side of the bed only for my hand to land on cold sheets. Ugh. Where is he? Squinting one eye, I look around the room, to find absolutely nothing. The walk-in closet door is open halfway, the light still on, but no sounds come from the room. He's not here.

Maybe he's downstairs curled up by the fire with his sketchbook. I roll out of bed, scratching at my bare stomach as I plod toward the bathroom. Once business is taken care of, it really starts to irk me that Reid didn't let me wake up with him in my arms, sassy and sleepy. My favorite kind of Reid.

After getting dressed, I descend the cold wood stairs in search of Reid. Scrolling through my phone, I glance up expecting to find him curled up in the chair by the fire, but there's no fire going, and notably no Reid. Well. Okay. I click through the app on my phone that shows his location, but the ring just shows him up in the bedroom. Now I'm starting to get nervous.

"He left a few hours ago," Hayden calls out from his perch at the dining table.

I jump a few inches in the air because I somehow didn't notice him. Hayden has that way about him. If he wants to be seen, you'll know it, otherwise he can easily blend into whatever room he's inhabiting.

"Any idea where he went?" I ask.

Hayden quirks one eyebrow as if to say *yes, but I'm not telling you*. I scowl his way which only earns me a laugh from Hayden. Prick. I trudge back up the stairs, irritated and annoyed, because I had a particular vision for how this Saturday morning was going to go. Wake up with sleepy, sassy Reid, roll him over and fuck him, then treat him like the little prince he is allllllllll day. But no, now he's gone and I'm left to my own devices.

Wiping at my eyes in frustration, I toss myself back on my bed, only to land on something crumbly and noisy. What. I reach under my back and pull out a now crumpled piece of paper with Reid's neat scroll across it. Oh.

Find me, asshole.

I SMILE DESPITE MYSELF. When I tilt my head to the side that's when I see the black ring on the nightstand. Oh, he wants to be found. Suddenly the day feels a lot more exciting than it did just a few moments ago. Jumping out of the bed, I race down the stairs, barely registering Hayden's delighted laugh in the kitchen. Tugging on my own thick jacket, I push out into the garage only to be greeted with an impatient-looking Parker.

"Jesus, that took you forever." He promptly tosses the keys at me and I catch them against my chest. "Onetime-*only* favor to use my car. If you return it with one scratch, you're a dead man. Also, Reid said something about being where he likes to be watched." Parker passes by me in a flurry of his warm-scented cologne. "You guys are weird. No fucking in the car."

Little does he know that now the idea has been planted. I won't be able to go on without fucking Reid at least once in the car. I climb into the car, start it, and sit for a minute to try to think up where he could be. The library? School's closed for winter break but maybe he could still get in.

The roads are lightly lined with snow as I drive toward the school. I love the hush that falls over the city with snow-fall. After growing up in New Mexico, snow was a new thing for me to get used to the past few years. Yeah, it took acclimating, but now I'm partial to the aesthetics of it. Although the reality is often infuriating, it's still worth the way the snow softens everything it touches.

The school parking lot is empty like I imagined it would be. Running through the snow is more dangerous than anything else, one bad step and my head gets cracked. The library door is unlocked when I push against it, warmth washing over me as I shake the snow out of my hair and wipe down my jacket. The usual front desk person is absent, some of the lights off, not even a security guard. Hopefully Reid doesn't get us expelled with this stunt.

I'm not sure where to start looking for him though.

I just start at the bottom and decide to work my way up.

Not wanting to turn lights on to draw attention to myself,

I use my phone flashlight to skulk through the first floor. The first floor of the library is mostly technical texts, research books that I haven't ever spent much time with.

Eerie silence greets me, despite the quiet slap of my feet against the carpeted floor. Once I've swept the first floor, I take the staircase to the second floor. I hope Reid doesn't make me look through all five floors only to find out this is the *wrong* location and he's actually waiting for me ass up somewhere else. As I sweep the second floor, I think about the last few weeks with Reid. He's become *such* a good boy for me when he's not hissing and spitting. I kind of want to take him home to meet my parents... and Ama. I want him to meet my family because he's my family now too. Reid's the one. No one else will ever match my crazy beat for beat but him. I think if I asked Reid to kill for me, he would, which is exactly the energy I'll need for this fucked-up world.

Imagining Reid in my parents' kitchen is easy, him helping my mom make dinner as my mom shares stories about me running naked through the neighborhood as a toddler. God, I want that so bad. I'm going to ask him the next time I see him. If I can fucking find him.

The emergency lights flicker on the third floor, making my breath hitch with the promise of finding Reid. It's still hush-quiet, but I can feel Reid close by, it's hard to explain. When he's near me, my body knows. I make my footfalls quieter, make my big body less conspicuous as I dip between the rows of books to hunt him down. The gentle flick of pages being turned reaches my ears as I edge toward the table he sat at all those weeks ago.

He's so fucking beautiful. He hasn't dyed his hair since we met, so there's a hefty growth of dark auburn at his roots. The hairs curl behind his ears, almost too overly long, falling into his face when he hunches down further to continue to search for whatever he wants to find in the book on the table. His thin fingers pause on a page, eyes crinkled at the corners as the very hint of a smile tips up his lips. He feels me too. We're connected like magnets, close proximity will always bring us together.

Reid sighs in frustration at not finding what he's seeking and stands abruptly, the chair scratching roughly against the carpet. I watch, heart pounding, as he heads the opposite way to return the book. He's dressed in my favorite outfit. Dark skinny jeans with a maroon sweater that shows a peek of his shoulder when he lifts the book to clutch it against his chest.

I dip into another row to keep my eye on him as he moves through the rows to find another book. Pausing halfway through the row, I watch as he lifts onto his tiptoes to return the current book, fingertips dancing across the books on a lower shelf as he drops back down to the soles of his feet. Even that is fucking elegant. He has no idea how much he's bewitched me. I think if I told him, he'd snarl and tell me to suck his dick, which I happily would, just to make him feel wanted.

He moves toward another row, but I don't think I can wait one more second to have him in my arms. Not to fuck him, not to suck his dick, but just to hold him and smell the warmth of his skin at the crook of his neck. Oh, I'm in so deep there's no coming back.

I sneak up behind him as he pauses at a shelf to stare up at a book he can't reach even on his tiptoes. Coming up behind him, I lean up and tap the offending book.

"This one?"

Reid tilts his head backwards to stare up at me, light blue eyes and pale skin, all sharp edges and desire. I don't give a fuck about the book. I drop my hand to curl my fingers behind his ear, holding his head so that he can't pull away.

"I wanted to wake up with you," I murmur close to his lips.

Reid smirks as he melts back against me. "Isn't this fun though?"

"I'm cold."

"I'll warm you up," Reid promises.

And then he crashes his lips against mine. He tastes like those damn cherry candies he's always sucking on, but no cigarettes because he hasn't smoked since the blowup with the twins. My good boy. I own Reid's mouth with my own, laying claim to him with my kiss.

"This is fun, but I really just want to take you home and fuck you in our bed," I say, sounding like a beggar even to my own ears.

"You've turned into a romantic so fast," Reid notes, not sounding remotely irritated though.

I nuzzle against the crook of his neck, my favorite spot on his body. Minus his ass. Kissing his pounding pulse, I curl my hands against his arms and hold him close to me where he belongs.

"I love you, Reid."

"I love you too, Dante," Reid says easily, like it costs him nothing.

"I wanna take you home over spring break to meet my family, to meet Ama."

Reid turns around in my arms to blink up at me, confusion, fear, and a little love shine in his eyes. "Really?"

"Yeah, will you come?"

Reid looks down at his feet, his telltale show of vulnerability. "I can't fly... we'd have to drive."

"I'll buy a camper. I don't give a fuck."

Reid chuckles, deep and low, before tilting up onto his tiptoes to kiss me soft and slow. "Alright, Dante. You can take me home. Well, over spring break, and now, because it's quite cold and I think I need you to warm me up."

My chest overflows with love and desire for him all at once. Wrapping my arm around his shoulder, I guide him down the stairs and out to the car with a grin on my face that feels natural, and real.

———

THE SNOW FALLS away after a few days, the air heating up enough to melt the slushy piles of snow scattered around campus. We're still in the throes of winter. When winter softens, maybe I'll whisk Reid away for a romantic stay in a cabin, just the two of us. Trudging out of the engineering building, I amble toward the math building to find Reid. It's easy for me to spot him in the distance, my eyes just naturally fall to him whenever they can. He's lying on his stomach in the quad, a blanket tossed over the still too-cold grass. Nobody else is out there, only Reid as he waits for me.

Two hurt people in a broken world finding one another at the exact right time. Maybe life is more than a string of happy accidents, maybe it's purposeful. Because I can't imagine a world where I'm not meant to find Reid, to love him, to hold him down and fuck him until he cries. The sun breaks through the clouds at the exact moment Reid lifts his head from his sketchbook to lock gazes with mine.

Reid promptly flips me off, happily returning his attention to his sketchbook. But the telltale smirk curving the edges of his lips tells me absolutely everything I need to know.

I think I'll call it love.

THE END... *for now.*

WANT MORE DANTE AND REID? Catch a glimpse of Reid's first official mission as part of the crew now.

You might be wondering who is next... well... I'm not much of a secret keeper so I'll spoil you now... Mason and Parker are coming this fall! Pre-order them now.

If you enjoyed this book please consider leaving a review wherever you feel most comfortable.

ACKNOWLEDGMENTS

This book is total wish fulfillment for me. There are so many times I wish I could be a part of a crew like Robin's boys. I'm an anarchist and anti-government gal at heart. This book wouldn't have happened without every person that has ever made a joke about me being on a government watchlist. If I wasn't before, I sure am now.

To JJ, thanks for being eager to read and support me in any way possible. You make everything so much *easier* just by being you. The next one's for you.

To Hannah, I know this one was totally out of your comfort zone. But you are a true friend in every way because you read it, loved them, and cheered me on when I was unsure.

To Lauren, Kristen, Lexi, Amber, and Donatella... thanks for always being up for a read even when I go a little farther than everyone expected. If I go back for Joey and Lee one day, it'll be because of y'all.

ABOUT THE AUTHOR

Maya spends most of her time imagining happily ever afters for the characters that live in her head. If she's not plotting how to heal broken hearts for her characters, then she's spending time with her precocious daughter. She loves baking competitions, listening to the same song on repeat for months, and discussing the latest pop culture event in a group chat with her best friends.